THE CHATTERBOX GIRL

THE CHATTERBOX GIRL

Elaine Carrier

Cover design and illustration by Maeve Norton.

Interior drawings by Isabelle Carrier

Editing by Timothy Bray and Lucille Carbonneau

Blog editing by Angelique Carrier and Gabrielle Carrier

This is a work of fiction. Names, characters, businesses, places, events, locales, and incidents are either the products of the author's imagination or used in a fictitious manner. Any resemblance to actual persons, living or dead, or actual events is purely coincidental.

This book is dedicated to my real-life Timothy

I would like to thank my husband Bill for his love, friendship and constant support during the writing of this book. Thank you to my family and friends for their encouragement. A special thanks to my mother Lucille and my brother Timothy who spent hours and days of their time editing and offering their valuable advice. Our editing sessions produced a lot of laughter and added to the fun of writing this story. Thank you to Maeve Norton for being a pleasure to work with and for sharing her exceptional talent, designing and illustrating my book cover. Thank you to my daughter Isabelle for her awesome interior illustrations and the fun and laughter we shared working together. Thank you to my daughters Angelique and Gabrielle for their help with my blog. Thank you to my wonderful cat Liam who was the inspiration for the character James. Although I lost him after 18 years, during the writing of this story, he will live on forever in Chatterbox World. Love to my cats, Cooper and Casey, my constant companions while writing and illustrating this book. All of the above mentioned made telling my story a wonderful experience.

Table of Contents

Phonetic spelling of the characters' names

Firinne (fear-ren-nay)

Gra (grah)

Searc (shark)

Eagla (E-glah)

Koko Lakiki (Koko Lah-kee-kee)

Mamo (Mam-moe)

Mr. Timpiste (Mr. Tim-pist)

CHAPTER 1

FIX-IT, SPARKLE AND POP

P oppy McGee was ten years old. She had light brown hair and blueberry eyes that were like windows to her soul. Hiding her emotions from the world was not a skill she was good at. Her blue eyes were underlined by a curvy row of freckles that marched across her nose. Her rosebud lips were quite tiny for her face, but big words and a lot of them came out of her mouth for most of her waking hours. She resented being called a chatterbox by a few of the kids at school. She just had a lot to say. Her imagination was as big as the collection of books she had in her bedroom.

Her bookshelves were overflowing and the tops of her dresser and desk were stacked with mysteries and adventures that expanded her imagination one book at a time. She inherited her love of reading and the feel of a book in her hand from her mother, who was an avid reader her whole life.

She was not very good at the social aspect of school. It was so hard to find the right clothes, pick the right shoes and say the right things. Sunday nights were especially agonizing for her. A stomach ache and a deep feeling of dread would consume Poppy as the day wore on and she found herself facing another week of school. She kept mostly to herself except when she was with her best friend Ella. Everything seemed easier when Ella was around. She could say what she meant and be herself with Ella, because what Poppy possessed in imagination, Ella could match with a heart of gold. Poppy didn't mind not fitting in at school too much, because what mattered most to her was the time she spent at home. Her school day was just something to get through and mostly a place where she'd meet up with Ella to make plans for their next adventure.

On this particular day, Poppy met Ella in the hallway at school. With just a glance at Poppy's face, Ella could tell that her friend was having a tough day.

"It's Friday," said Ella with an encouraging smile.

Poppy gave her sweet friend a weak smile as she blinked black the tears that were flooding her baby blues.

"You're getting off the bus at my house?" squeaked Poppy, her voice trying to adjust itself to her feelings.

"You betcha Pops!" Ella said enthusiastically with a huge grin. "Gonna be a great weekend. I can feel it in me bones!" she joked, her eyes sparkling with laughter.

This made Poppy smile and almost forget her troubled day, because experience had shown that Ella's bones and how they felt were a good indicator of what was to come.

The rest of the school day went by uneventfully and soon Poppy was sitting beside Ella on the school bus, spilling out her tale of woe, describing in detail about how Gwen Grotty, Bonnie Craven and Karlyn Keister had whispered to each other all during art class, glancing at her and laughing. She felt sure that they were once again making fun of her favorite denim overalls. The only breath that Poppy took as she chattered on, was when the bus collided with an oversized pothole, causing her to take a deep breath and open her eyes wide. But she collected herself and finished her story with a very exaggerated sigh. Ella patiently listened to her dear friend, shaking her head and scrunching her face up in disapproval, which warmed Poppy's heart. This was all that Poppy needed. Her true and loyal friend, who not always agreed with her, but was there to listen and usually say something to make her feel better. They sat in silence as the bus made its stops and starts. Finally, Ella broke the silence by saying;

"Poppy, you can't let them upset you. They pick on you only because they can see it bothers you so much. You need to grow a turtle shell Pops. You've got to shut them out. You can do it Poppy."

She looked straight into Poppy's eyes with that special sparkle and grinned like only Ella could, from ear to ear, just like a Cheshire cat. And that was the last time they even thought about school or Gwen Grotty, Bonnie Craven or Karlyn Keister; well at least until dinnertime.

Poppy lived in a rambling old farmhouse on the outskirts of town. She shared her home with her father Seamus, her older brother Finn, her grandmother, who was lovingly called Mamo, and their clever dog Toby. The house had been in her father's family for generations. It was situated on a country road that ended with a large field, and thick woods beyond. Vintage oversized rocking chairs and a porch swing were residents of its large wraparound porch. Most of the furnishings were old and passed down through the family. Mismatched and worn furniture mixed in with newer pieces added throughout the years, gave the home a comfortable feel. Thick dark beams, hewn from the trees cut down to build the home, supported the ceilings of the house. In the kitchen, beautiful hand-woven baskets hung from the heavy beams, each one containing useful cooking items and treats out of reach of the children. An enormous fieldstone fireplace lined the wall in the living room and offered comfort and warmth during the winter months. Opposite the fireplace were floor to ceiling bookcases filled to capacity with her mother's treasured books, old and new.

Poppy had lost her mother to cancer when she was five years old, but her mother's beauty, her love of reading and the special loving touches she added to the home were still very much a part of their lives. The rest of the first floor contained Mamo's sewing room, their father's office, Finn's workshop and a long sun room with many windows facing the back field.

When he was not traveling for business, Poppy's father Seamus, a successful attorney, spent most of his time in his office which was also lined with shelves, but for a different reason. Seamus was a lover of music. His shelving was filled with classic rock, blues and jazz record albums. In the center of his office stood a beautiful vintage Victrola record player. It was a treasure passed down to him by his grandfather. The case was made of dark cherry wood. One of Poppy's earliest memories, was of her father holding her in his arms as they wound the crank on the side of the old Victrola. He let her push the silver lever which started rotating the felted turntable. Then Seamus would place the steel needle onto the thick disc. After a few quiet popping noises, the needle slid its way around the grooves of the thick 78 rpm records, playing the melodies of old. Her father would dance around the room as Poppy giggled and flapped her arms to the music.

The soft tones of Ella Fitzgerald, the gravelly voice and lively horn of Louis Armstrong and the piano magic of Jelly Roll Morton could usually be heard drifting from the room, while Seamus poured over the details of his next client's case. Poppy's father was known for his easy-going disposition and quiet demeanor, which to the surprise of his clients completely changed when he was in the courtroom. It is here that he overpowered his adversaries with his aggressive attack supported by his intellect and thorough research. His ability to put the jury at ease and then mesmerize them with his power of persuasion was matched by few. His career consumed most of his schedule, but the time he spent with his family at the farmhouse was what filled his heart and soul with the strength and courage to perform in the courtroom.

****

The everyday struggle with the loss of his mother was not what defined Poppy's older brother, Finn. It was what this struggle had done to reshape who he was that was important. Perhaps it was just this that made him so good at fixing things. He was drawn to anything that was broken or stuck or needed to be helped to be whole and useful in some way. It started when he was very young. He had a toy stuffed tiger that was special to him. He felt connected to Tiger and his stripes. Every night before bed he would tell Tiger to guard the door to his room while he slept. He would place Tiger on the edge of the bed being careful to make sure the feline's little green glass eyes were aimed at his doorway. With the comfort of knowing Tiger was there by his side, he would dream the night away in peace.

One bright sunny morning, when Finn was in second grade, he woke to find that Tiger was gone from his bed. Rubbing his eyes and clearing away the remnants of dreams, he searched through his covers for his faithful striped friend. Starting to worry, Finn placed his bare feet on the floor and crouched down to look under his bed. Not finding

Tiger there or anywhere in his bedroom, Finn began to search the house for his little pal. Getting over excited by the thought of never seeing Tiger again, he started to run from room to room and plowed straight into his grandmother's white apron front.

"Hi Mamo!" he half panted half yelled to his grandmother. "I'm looking for Tiger. I can't find him anywhere!"

"Has he escaped from your room again?" she asked with a small laugh. "Why don't you check with Toby? You know how Toby *loves* to play hide and seek with Tiger."

"Oh no, not again!" groaned Finn.

Toby was Finn's lovable border collie. He was as smart as he was loyal to both Finn and Poppy. However, he had a bad habit of stealing Tiger and hiding him in various places. It was as if the mischievous dog knew the ruckus this would cause, and he seemed to enjoy jumping in on the search for Tiger. Finn ran through the large rambling farmhouse, making his way to the back door that led to a beautiful field of wildflowers and grass, spotted by various outbuildings. Placing his thumb and index finger in his mouth, Finn whistled, just like his mother's brother, Uncle Ernie, had taught him. It was a very loud shrill whistle that he was extremely proud of. It had taken him two whole weeks of practicing to perfect it but it was worth his time, because now he was the only one in the family besides Uncle Ernie that could produce such an impressive sound.

Finn was already very popular at school, and his whistling ability had earned him even more respect and admiration in the school yard this year and that was just fine with Finn.

It was only a few seconds after Finn whistled, that Toby came crashing through the grass and flowers at full speed wagging his tail and barking.

"You scoundrel Toby!" Finn said with a disapproving look. "What did you do with Tiger *now*?"

Toby circled around and around Finn, and then crashed down onto the grass still wagging his tail and looking excitedly at the boy's face.

"What were you doing out at the chicken house?" asked Finn suspiciously. "I'll beat you there!" he shouted to the dog, as he took off across the yard toward the little chicken shed. Toby was so enthusiastic for the chase, that he raced after the boy and almost knocked him over as he sprinted by and beat him to the shed. Toby stood in front of the door blocking Finn's entry.

"Ok I know where you hid him. Out of the way you rat!" laughed Finn. He pushed Toby aside and slid the makeshift wooden bar off the latch and entered the coop, scaring the chickens and causing them to run in all directions.

Toby didn't bother with the door. He crouched down and pushed his way into the chicken house by means of the hole in the ground he had dug underneath. He much preferred his self-made entrance and used it often to sneak into the coop for an afternoon snooze. Searching in all the nests and under the straw, Finn attempted to find Tiger, but came up empty. He crashed to the floor and started wondering if he'd made a mistake about finding Tiger in the chicken house, when something caught his eye. The sun was reflecting on Tiger's little green glass eye as he hung crookedly off the windowsill. With one bound, Finn jumped from the floor and grabbed his beloved Tiger and hugged him with all his strength. It was just then that he saw one of Tiger's eyes hanging by just a single thread.

"Oh no," moaned Finn. "Toby you were too rough with Tiger. You wrecked one of his eyes!" he said angrily to the dog.

The look on Toby's furry mug made it clear that the dog knew he was in trouble. Toby made a whining noise and gave Finn his big eyed "I'm sorry" face. The guilty dog followed Finn as he walked slowly back to the house, making sure not to drop the dangling eye. Slamming the screen door behind him, Finn called out for his grandmother and held the one-eyed tiger in front of her.

"One of Tiger's eyes is loose Mamo. Can I borrow your sewing thread and needle to fix it?"

Mamo took the little tiger in her hands and felt the soft striped fur between her fingers.

"Of course, you can Finn," she said with a warm smile. "Follow me."

Finn and Toby tagged along behind Mamo until they reached her little sewing room. The room was cozy, with an old easy chair in one corner where Mamo did her hand sewing and a work table on the other side where she kept her sewing machine. Mamo always kept everything very tidy and all her sewing supplies were lined up on the table in a special order.

"Thanks, Mamo. I'll be sure to put everything back exactly as I found it," Finn said with a loving smile.

He hugged his grandmother around the waist and closed his eyes and smiled. She was always there, willing to help, and her light-hearted manner made Finn feel happy. While Mamo made her way back to the kitchen to finish preparing the wonderful smelling cookies she was baking, Finn sat down in Mamo's easy chair and started sewing the little glass eye back onto Tiger's face. He knew how to sew at this early age, as well as many other useful things, because instead of doing things for Finn, his mother and Mamo had always felt it more useful to teach him to do things for himself. In doing this, they had given Finn the gift of independence, self-esteem and courage, which would last him his whole life. Finn's mother felt very strongly that it was important for her children to accomplish things on their own, especially teaching them that to do something well, one must try and fail and try again to be successful.

Toby looked quite comical as he watched Finn do the repairs. The dog's eyes were glued to the little needle as Finn pushed it into Tiger's fur and then pulled back through the air with each stitch. He looked hopefully at Finn when the repair was complete and was rewarded with a pat on the head.

Carefully replacing each of Mamo's sewing tools exactly where he found them, Finn decided he and Toby should go explore the winding river that snaked through the field out back, and perhaps make a little boat for Tiger.

Several years had passed since Tiger's eye surgery and Finn now had a special room in the sprawling farmhouse that he could call his very own workshop. It was one of his favorite places to be. He had learned so much from Mamo and from his mother's brother, Uncle Ernie, who was a mechanic in town. Ernie was a "jack of all trades" as one might say. He was very good with his hands and had learned the skill of repairing cars at technical school when he was young. He was also a master welder and had a fair knowledge of carpentry and masonry. Ernie was very outgoing and knew almost everyone in town, since they all relied on him to repair their cars or tractors. Many of his customers were laborers and were glad to trade services as payment. Ernie always enjoyed his nephew's company and was surprised at how much the young boy was interested in fixing things and more amazed at how quickly he learned.

As soon as he got home from school and had checked in with Mamo, Finn hopped on his bike and made short work of the mile into town. He leaned his bike under the sign Ernie's Repair and Weld, and walked into the shop causing the old bell on the door to ring loudly. Ernie, sporting his usual well-worn coveralls, slid out from under an old jeep.

"What have you been up to lately?" asked Ernie, cleaning his hands off with a rag.

"Just got home from school and I thought I would come say hi," Finn said grinning. "You have any projects you need a hand with?"

Before Ernie could answer Finn, the antique bell noisily shook again and in walked family friend, Mr. Timpiste, a retired veteran who was the sole proprietor of a local repair shop, named Contraption Rehab. Mr. Timpiste was glad to see Finn's smiling face. Finn loved nothing better than to help the older veteran in his little store and Mr. Timpiste loved the boy's company and the extra hand with the work load. He did quite well with his fix-it business because he was good at repairing mostly everything. He was also secretly grateful to teach someone who was genuinely interested and marveled at how kind, respectful and intelligent the boy was. He was deeply saddened that Finn had lost his mother at such an early age and was glad to offer the boy a diversion from the loss, and something positive to fill his mind.

Mr. Timpiste, who had been in the military, had led a quiet singular life as a transport pilot in Alaska for many years, until he retired to his hometown of Tibbard. Finn admired Mr. Timpiste very much and he loved to listen to stories of his travels while in the service and as a pilot transporting freight, mail and passengers in Alaska.

Mr. Timpiste nodded a hello to Ernie.

"I have an old wind up clock in for repair," Mr. Timpiste told Finn. "I know clocks are your favorite," he said with a small smile.

Finn was very excited at the thought of disassembling the clock. Mr. Timpiste had taught him how to take them apart, clean the gears and the main spring, check the bushings for wear and put them back together again. Finn was not ready to do the work on his own but with Mr. Timpiste's patient guidance he was on his way to being able to work independently.

"Can we go to the shop right now and start Mr. Timpiste?" Finn asked eagerly.

"I'm pretty much done for the day. How 'bout we start first thing in the morning?"

"Ok," Finn answered with a smile.

He was excited to have a new mission for Saturday morning since his plans to play street hockey with his friends from school had fallen through. His two best buddies, Mike Muggins and Charlie Stubbs, had broken a window at school while playing baseball, and their Saturdays were now filled with chores and small jobs for the neighbors, earning money to pay for the damage. Both Mike and Charlie lived in the Berry Street Neighborhood. They had become friends a week after Charlie moved into the ranch house across the street from Mike. It was Charlie's 5th birthday and his backyard party included pin the tail on the donkey, a puppet show, bobbing for apples, duck-duck-goose, and best of all, a wild west fight with real cap guns. Mike left the party with chocolate cake smeared on his smiling face, feeling very confident that life was definitely better than it was only a week ago.

By the end of second grade, Finn had become great friends with Mike and Charlie and now that they were in sixth grade they had become inseparable. Finn was very popular, with his good looks and outgoing personality. He was tall and lanky for his age, with dark brown curly hair and walnut brown eyes that made the girls blush, that is, when they got the courage to talk to him. A lot of the kids called him "Fix-It-Finn" because it was well known that he hung around with his Uncle Ernie and Mr. Timpiste and was good at fixing things like they were. Mike was tall for his age, thin and wiry, with unruly black hair and a signature broken front tooth, which he acquired during an infamous after school fight with Gwenn Grotty's older brother Greg. Greg was a year older than Mike but the fight ended with a whimpering, black eyed, bloody nosed Grotty running off while the crowd of kids circled Mike, chanting MUGGINS! MUGGINS! MUGGINS! They were all pretty excited that someone had finally stood up to the bully. Charlie and Finn were very proud of their friend, but Charlie already knew that Mike was as loyal as he was tough. Charlie was on the small side for his class, a little more rounded, his face covered in freckles that rimmed his blue eyes. It was an unspoken rule that no one bothered Charlie or they'd have to answer to Mike.

Finn, Charlie and Mike organized the Berry Street neighborhood weekend games, so without Mike and Charlie there to set things up, their Saturday street hockey and baseball would have to go on hold.

Finn spent an hour or so watching Ernie work on the jeep's engine and listening to Ernie and Mr. Timpiste swap tales about what was going on in town. Before Finn left on his bike, Ernie brought out three bottles of soda from the Super Fizz Soda Factory, a small family run business in town that prided themselves on having the fizziest soda with the most unusual names. Finn drank down his favorite Gargantuan Grape, while Ernie enjoyed Supercilious Strawberry and Mr. Timpiste finished off his Sonic Sarsaparilla.

****

Poppy McGee met Ella Mansfield in first grade. While Poppy squeezed her father, Seamus' hand and attempted to become part of his leg so that he couldn't leave without her, Ella scoped out the classroom for the best seat and the desk with the coolest pencil case. Each desk was topped with a workbook and a brand-new case filled with supplies, and Ella was currently eyeing the bright purple case with yellow daisies on it. Her sparkling brown eyes and smooth tan skin were outdone by the cascading deep brown ringlets that framed her face. She maintained a smug look of confidence and a gleam in her eye as she scanned the room filled with her new classmates. Most of them looked frightened and wary of their new classroom, but no one looked more despondent then the girl with two long braids connected by a row of bangs, clinging to her father's leg. Ella's dad, Miles Mansfield was talking to Poppy's dad, Seamus McGee. They were both lawyers and friendly since they knew each other from court. Seamus didn't seem to even notice his daughter's tight grip or that she had wrapped herself around his legs. Ella suddenly noticed that in the right hand of the frightened girl was a *Star Trek* lunchbox. Ella knew in that moment, they would become good friends.

"*I mean Star Trek is the coolest,*" she thought. "*What other girl likes Star Trek?*" Ella had seen plenty of girly lunchboxes in her time, but "*this girl really knows a good show when she sees one,*" she mumbled, approaching Poppy.

"Hi! I'm Ella," she said flashing a smile at Poppy. "Nice lunch box. Have you seen the 'Trouble with Tribbles' episode?"

Poppy loosened her grip on her father's leg and the two girls began to chat about their favorite *Star Trek* episodes. Poppy told Ella that she watched the show with her brother Finn, and that Ella should come over and watch it together with them sometime.

"I'll have to ask my dad. It's our special show. We never miss an episode," Ella replied.

"Ok with me Sparkle," said Ella's father, Miles, using his special nickname for his little girl with the sparkling eyes.

Both Seamus McGee and Miles Mansfield seemed amused at the conversation their daughters were having. Ella suggested that she and Poppy claim the two best pencil cases, which happened to be on two desks in the front row next to one another.

Within weeks the girls were inseparable. They spent time after school at Ella's house, an impressive colonial built in the 1800's with a front porch on 369 Main Street.

Seamus was glad to see his daughter getting out of the house and socializing. Since her mother's death, Poppy didn't seem to want to leave home, and spent most of her time with Mamo and Finn. It was good to see Poppy smiling again. He hoped that her time spent with Ella would lesson her feelings of loss and sadness, and rid her of the nightmares she had been having.

Poppy loved the liveliness of being downtown. After school, as they got older, she and Ella would walk to Lucy's Diner, only a few doors down, to get a snack and drink. They felt very grown up doing this by themselves.

Every Wednesday Ella would have her piano lesson on the beautiful grand piano in the lavish living room at 369 Main. Poppy was there to observe. When Ella practiced before her lesson, Poppy was her audience, clapping at the end of each piece and giving three rounds of Bravo when Ella didn't make any mistakes. Sometimes Ella made her stay out on the front porch while she practiced because Poppy's enthusiasm made it hard to concentrate.

Ella Mansfield's mom was very kind to Poppy, and many evenings when Poppy's father, Seamus, needed to stay late at work, Poppy would be invited to dinner. Sometimes, while Ella practiced her piano, Mrs. Mansfield would listen to Poppy tell her about what had happened at school that day and who said what and why and when. Poppy had a lot to say and Ella's mom was a good listener. Poppy was also sure to tell Mrs. Mansfield, that she loved the fine china and the beautiful chandelier that hung over the dining room table. A little smile formed on Mrs. Mansfield's face when she overheard Poppy very confidently tell Ella that, "although she loved living in a country farmhouse, being at her house was like visiting the castles in her story books."

Poppy McGee and Ella Mansfield were now almost finished with fifth grade and the school summer break of 1975 was almost upon them. Poppy was counting down the weeks to the end of the school year. On most Fridays, Ella would ride the bus to Poppy's house. She would sleep over and spend the weekend with the McGee family. This was a real treat for Mamo because she was very fond of Ella and Ella loved Mamo *and* her cooking. On this particular Friday, Mamo made the girls' favorite dinner of lasagna made from her special secret recipe, a salad with fresh vegetables delivered by Uncle Ernie that very morning, homemade bread, and apple crisp with ice cream for dessert. Mamo loved listening to Finn, Ella and especially Poppy talk a mile a minute about their week at school and their plans for the weekend.

Finn agreed with Ella, that Gwen Grotty, Bonnie Craven and Karlyn Keister were simply picking on Poppy because they could see how much it bothered her. He offered his services along with those of his two friends, Mike Muggins and Charlie Stubbs, to have a word with the prickly girls, but Ella quickly shot him down since she wasn't confident she knew what "have a word" quite meant.

"I think she's all set," she said raising her eyebrows and giving Finn a look, which made him squirm.

"Well they're a nasty bunch," said Finn shaking his head. "Mike and Charlie said they saw them downtown the other day chasing Mr. Timpiste's cat around the yard. The poor cat was nearly hit by a car as she ran into the road to get away from them."

Poppy's face began to turn red at the thought of those wretched girls but Ella abruptly changed the mood.

"Toby!" she shrieked jumping off her seat and crawling onto the floor to give the dog a hug. Ella adored Toby and wished she could have a dog at her house but mom was allergic and that was that.

"Finn," Ella crooned in her sweetest voice, "can Toby sleep with me and Poppy tonight?"

"Be my guest!" said Finn rolling his eyes. "At least I won't have to look for Tiger in the morning if he's busy with you two."

Poppy and Ella giggled because they both knew how much Toby loved to steal and hide Tiger.

"Thanks for dinner Mamo!" they all shouted at once, which made them laugh and made Mamo grin.

"We'll do the dishes Mamo," Ella said kindly. "That way you can sit and rest and tell us about *your* day!"

"Well, most of it was spent cooking and baking, which is fine with me. But one thing I noticed when I went out to the chicken house to get eggs was that the river sounded very high, so you kids should be careful when you're out there tomorrow," Mamo cautioned. "Another strange thing I heard was a meowing," said Mamo in a quiet thoughtful voice. "There might be a kitty out there that is hungry or lost. Keep an eye out and bring it to the back door for some milk and tuna if you can."

"Ok Mamo will do," said Poppy.

The rest of the dishwashing session was filled with Finn poking Ella in the side while dodging her swinging arms as she tried to smack him away.

"Ok that's enough helping," said Mamo. "Make sure everything is put back in its place and then go have some fun."

CHAPTER 2

A CURIOUS CAT

The next morning, Finn left early on his bike to meet Mr. Timpiste at Contraption Rehab. He was looking forward to working on the clock repairs and trying out some new tools.

Meanwhile Poppy and Ella, carrying the lunch basket prepared for them by Mamo, headed out to the back field to sit by the river and make plans for the day. Of course, Toby had come along to supervise and guard their picnic basket, but before long he wandered off sniffing the trail of something a little more interesting than peanut butter sandwiches. Out of the corner of her eye,

Poppy caught sight of something moving on the other side of the river. She scrambled to her feet and shaded her eyes to see what it was.

"What do you see over there, Pops?" Ella asked jumping up to look.

"It's an orange tiger cat!" squealed Poppy.

The very large tiger cat was now sitting on the bank of the river on the opposite side. He was staring very intently at the girls.

"Let's go see him," Poppy said softly to Ella as to not scare the cat away; although the dull roar of the river this time of year would most certainly have blocked the sound of her voice. Poppy and Ella made their way down to the bridge that passed over the river at its narrowest point. They quietly crossed keeping their eyes on the orange tiger cat, who in turn kept his eyes on them. Once they were on the other side, they slowly and quietly approached the cat, calling out to it. Just when they thought they would be able to reach him without scaring him away, Toby appeared out of nowhere barking and running toward the cat. Ella and Poppy were sure that the cat would run off as soon as he heard Toby, but strangely the cat remained quite still, now steadily gazing at the approaching dog. Bounding up to within one foot of the cat, Toby came to a skidding stop and laid flat on the ground. The girls were frozen in place waiting to see what would happen next. Nothing happened.

The cat stared at Toby. Toby stared at the cat. The girls' gaze bounced between Toby and the cat and then to each other. Nobody moved. Finally, Poppy growled at Toby, telling him to get lost, but the dog simply cocked his head to one side and then the other. Both girls stood up, eased their way toward Toby and then sat on the ground with their legs crossed.

"You're a strange kitty," Ella said breaking the silence.

The cat shifted his eyes, which incidentally matched the color of his fur, to Ella's face.

"Is that a smirk he has on his face?" Ella asked Poppy with a slight tremor in her voice.

"Sure looks like one," Poppy said matter-of-factly.

"Hey Mr. Kitty," said Ella sweetly, deciding to change her tactic. "Are you lost and hungry?"

The cat blinked both eyes at Ella, stood up and started to walk away from them toward the woods beyond the field.

"Let's follow him Ella!" suggested Poppy enthusiastically. "Let's see where he's going."

"I don't know," answered Ella shaking her head with uncertainty. Mamo and Seamus always told us not to go further than the edge of the field."

"Well we can follow him to the edge then," urged Poppy.

"But Pops…," Ella started to argue.

26

Poppy was already running ahead to catch up with the strange cat. Ella ran after her, pleading with her to stop.

"We can't Pops! We can't go into the woods. We're not supposed to!" Ella whined.

"We'll be Ok," Poppy reassured Ella. "We have Toby with us and we can still see the house from here."

Ella looked behind her to check for Toby, only to find the dog was sitting nervously behind her, looking just as unsure as she was.

"Toby's acting very strangely," Ella said scrunching up her face with concern. "Why isn't he chasing this cat? Why isn't the cat afraid of him? Toby loves to chase cats, birds, squirrels and *everything else* in this field!!" Ella said incredulously.

"I'm not sure," Poppy answered shrugging her shoulders. "That's why I want to follow the cat!" She opened her eyes as big as she could and held her breath waiting for Ella's answer.

Just at this moment they both heard a loud meowing coming from somewhere ahead among the trees. Ella reached out and grabbed Poppy's hand and together they made their way between the towering pine trees that loomed high over their heads. Within a few seconds they caught sight of the tiger cat. His orange and white fur coat was easy to see among the dark colors of the woods. Although the sun was shining brightly this

Saturday morning, most of the bright rays were hidden by the canopy above. The cat didn't seem to be in any particular hurry and the girls and Toby followed closely behind. After about ten minutes, just when the girls started to lose their nerve and wish they had listened to Mamo and Seamus, the cat suddenly sat down. He was still facing away from them. He didn't turn around. He simply sat and gazed into the forest in front of them.

"*Now* what do we do?" Ella pleaded, holding her arms out in frustration. "We just followed a cat into the woods for no reason. He's not even going anywhere in particular."

Poppy, Ella and Toby all sat on the pine needle floor watching the cat.

"Where *are* you going Mr. Cat?" Poppy asked. "Let's go back to our house for some milk and tuna," she said encouragingly.

But the cat sat very still gazing at the woods still ahead. Poppy and Ella both craned their necks to see what the cat was looking at. Poppy stood up and walked over to the tangled mess of brush that the cat's eyes were fixed upon. Gathering a clump of vines in her hand she pushed them to one side and gasped, "Ella, come here!"

CHAPTER 3

THE OCTAGONAL CABIN

It stood alone in the middle of the forest, hidden from anyone who wasn't really looking for it. Creeping vines had slowly slipped around the corners of its roof and wrapped their gnarled fingers around the little house. It was surrounded by very old trees, that had witnessed years of comings and goings. They seemed to watch over the tiny structure. On sunny days, shimmering rays of sunlight snuck between the branches of the towering tree giants and danced upon the little patches of roof, which poked through the vines. On rainy days, if you listened closely, you could hear the tapping of raindrops on the red tin roof. On this particular day, the woods were exceptionally quiet, as if the animals and trees and even the house itself were holding their breath. Something was about to happen; something that had not happened in a very long time. The little house would no longer be sad. The loneliness, which surrounded the house as thick as the creeping vines, would loosen its grasp. It was going to be a good day.

"Hurry up Ella!" Poppy whispered with an excited squeak.

Ella was jumping up and down on one leg trying to get into her jeans as quickly as possible. She was already wearing her favorite Dr. Pepper t-shirt. Poppy had finished slipping into her favorite comfy overalls and a plain white t-shirt she stole from Finn's room, and was weaving her long hair into two braids. The girls were so excited to go back into the woods to try and figure out what they had found in the waning hours of the previous afternoon. Yesterday in their excitement, it was surprising they had remembered to pick up their picnic basket, before chasing Toby back to the farmhouse. They arrived just in time for Mamo's delicious shepherd's pie.

"Where have you two been?" Mamo had asked as the girls came crashing back into the kitchen.

"You have fun out by the river today? Did you see that kitty I was telling you about?"

Poppy and Ella had given each other a sideways glance.

"The river is really high like you said Mamo," Poppy had answered, trying to avoid the subject of the cat.

"O my goodness you didn't eat a single thing from your picnic basket!"

"We were having so much fun playing with Toby we forgot to eat," Poppy had explained, hoping the subject would drop with that. "We're *starving*!" Poppy had said very dramatically.

"Yeah *really* starving" chimed in Ella.

Both girls had run off to wash their hands for dinner. Luckily Uncle Ernie and Finn had just arrived with some special treats from the Stibbard Bakery for Sunday morning breakfast. Finn had also brought home a box of Mr. Timpiste's homemade cookies that he made every Saturday for Mamo and the kids. Ernie stayed for dinner and the conversation was mostly about Ernie and Finn's day downtown, and details about Finn's new knowledge of mainsprings, and how to keep them from violently unwinding while he was working on a clock. Finn had certainly been doubly excited about meeting Ernie for a fizzy soda after he and Mr. Timpiste had closed the shop for the day.

As soon as they both were dressed and Poppy packed a few essential items into her backpack, they snuck quietly downstairs to see if Mamo was in the kitchen. The delicious donuts and muffins that Uncle Ernie brought over the night before were on the table in a basket, but Mamo was not in sight. Poppy and Ella each grabbed a donut and started to head for the door, when Mamo walked into the kitchen.

"You two are headed out early," she said with a laugh. "Out for more fun by the river? You better take sweatshirts. It might cool off later this afternoon."

"Ok Mamo!" shouted Poppy as she ran up the stairs to her room.

"Here Ella, take the picnic basket again. I've added two more donuts, some milk and sandwiches and of course some of Mr. Timpiste's cookies; unless you two want to come back and have lunch with me?"

"I think we're all set Mamo," said Poppy as she returned with two sweatshirts. "We have some adventuring to do. Thanks for being the best Mamo in the world!" she said with a toothy smile. Mamo smiled too and held her arms out to the girls.

"I love you two pumpkins," she said hugging them closely. "Be safe and check in with me in a few hours. You worried me a little yesterday."

Those were the last words the girls heard before they bolted out the door and ran across the back field. When they arrived at the bridge they slowed down to catch their breath. Shading their eyes against the bright sun, they scanned the area they had last seen the tiger cat.

"He kinda gives me the jitters," mumbled Ella.

"He's just a silly cat," Poppy laughed.

"I could have sworn he had a smirk on his face every time we tried to talk to him yesterday," Ella mused with a concerned look.

"Come on. Let's eat our donuts on the bridge. That way we can keep an eye out for him if he's around."

"Good idea," said Ella.

The two girls sat in silence eating their donuts and drinking out of the two small cartons of milk Mamo had packed in their basket. They kept a close watch on the edge of the field where they had seen the cat yesterday afternoon, while the noise of the river rumbled below.

"We need some tools," Ella said breaking the silence, "to cut away the vines and clear off whatever is under the brush."

"Definitely," Poppy said as she finished her donut.

They headed back to the tool shed that lived next to the chicken house.

"I found some clippers and an old iron rake. What else do you think we need?" asked Poppy from the back of the tool shed.

"We could probably use another set of pruners," suggested Ella. "We have a lot of brush and vines to get through."

They both searched around the dirt floored shed and finally found a second set of shears. Zipping the smaller tools into Poppy's backpack, they ran back to the bridge, Ella dragging the steel rake behind her. Just after crossing the river, Ella saw a splash of orange near the edge of the woods.

"He's there! Over there! I see the cat!" Ella shouted over the roar of the river water.

They took off in the direction of the cat, no longer worried it would run away from them. The girls stopped abruptly about a foot in front of the orange tiger.

"He's got that smirk on his face again!" Ella squeaked in a very high voice.

Poppy reached out and tried to pet the cat on his big furry orange striped head. The cat stepped backward squinting his eyes and shaking his head.

"Is he *really*, honestly shaking his head no?" Ella asked incredulously.

Poppy burst out laughing.

Mr. Cat flipped around suddenly and sprinted off toward the woods.

"Let's go!" shouted Poppy as she and Ella both trotted after the cat. Just as they left the field and entered the woods, Toby came bounding after them barking and wagging his tail.

"Where have you been hiding, Toby?" Poppy asked the pup as she and Ella caught up to the cat. "Is this the right place? Is this where we were yesterday?" Poppy wondered aloud.

"I think so," said Ella, concentrating on following the cat's gaze into the woods. "I see a little patch of red up among the vines. Look up there!" said Ella, pointing up toward the tangled mess.

"Ok, I'll clip the vines and you pull them away with the rake," instructed Poppy.

They worked very hard for about a half hour or so and found they had uncovered a stone wall.

"What do you think it is?" asked Poppy tapping on the wall.

"Let's take a rest," said Ella. "I'm sweating like a snowman in summer!"

"Yeah, we're definitely not gonna need these sweatshirts!"

Ella and Poppy rested for a while, sharing their sandwiches and cookies with Toby. The tiger cat was nowhere to be seen. They spent the next few hours clipping away the vines and dragging them off with the rake, taking turns and resting. When the afternoon sun started to fall to the West and they didn't have much energy left, they linked arms and surveyed what they had uncovered.

"Well it looks like a little house. A house made of stone."

"With a red roof," Poppy chimed in.

"All that work…. and we've uncovered only a piece of it!" Ella said wearily.

"I wonder what's inside," Poppy half whispered to Ella.

"We better head back," warned Ella. "Mamo will be looking for us."

Toby barked in agreement.

"Let's store our tools here until we can come back Pops."

"Good idea El."

After sliding their tools under the pile of vines they had discarded, Ella and Poppy slowly made their way back to the house.

"Too bad it's Sunday," Poppy moaned. "All I can think of is uncovering the house and exploring inside. I can't believe we have a whole week of school until we can come back."

"But you're forgetting something Pops! We have a three-day weekend coming up and I'm staying with you all weekend while my parents visit my grandma!"

Poppy inhaled sharply and jumped up and down squealing, her face glowing and her eyes as big as quarters.

"Calm down!" said Ella. "You're going to blow a gasket!" she shouted while laughing and running toward the house.

The following week of school felt like a month to Poppy.

"It's driving me craaaazy," Poppy moaned to Ella in the school cafeteria on Tuesday. "I'll *never* ever make it to Friday," she said, dramatically rolling her eyes.

"Pops you're so impatient... but I'm going a little nuts too. I can't stop thinking about exploring inside the house."

"What house?" asked Finn sliding onto the bench next to Ella.

"Tell him," Poppy said very seriously. "We need to tell him. We need his help to uncover it and who knows if it's locked!" she growled with a hushed voice.

Ella and Poppy both leaned toward Finn and with excited whispers, told him about discovering the orange tiger cat, following him into the woods and the little house they had uncovered.

"Whoa!" said Finn, with a new admiration for the girls mixed with excitement about being let in on their secret. "I'm in. I'll help you uncover the rest," he told them, his mind racing with plans. "You want me to ask Mike and Charlie to help too?"

"Well, I don't know," said Poppy scrunching up her face with worry. "Can we trust them with our secret? Mamo and Seamus would be really angry if they knew we had left the field. I'd just die if they found out!" Poppy said shaking her head fearfully.

"Let me come up with a plan," Finn stated confidently. "I won't mess it up, and it will give you a better chance of spending a lot of time outside if Mamo knows you're with me. She won't worry. She trusts me to take care of you, so we can spend more time in the woods, as long as we're back for supper."

Poppy and Ella were glad they had told Finn and were starting to feel more confident about their plans. Poppy breathed a sigh of relief and she and Ella said they would check in with Finn in a few days to firm up their plans for the weekend.

Wednesday after school, Finn met up with Mike and Charlie and a bunch of his other friends at the park to play baseball. Meanwhile, Poppy and Ella walked the block to Ella's house, stopping at Lucy's Diner for an Orange Fanta and French fries.

"We can tell Mamo that we're hanging out with Finn and store all our stuff in the back of the tool shed," said Ella.

"Yeah," agreed Poppy. "We'll need plenty to drink and work gloves."

"And a flashlight," added Ella, "in case there's no light inside."

"Good thinking Ella," said Poppy with a smile.

"Let's go. My piano teacher will be at the house soon."

With that they left, excited for their upcoming adventure.

After a delicious supper of beef stew and biscuits on Thursday night, Poppy and Finn hung out in Finn's workshop. While he worked on a cuckoo clock that Mr. Timpiste had entrusted him to fix, Poppy danced and twirled in circles to "Sister Golden Hair" by her favorite group *America,* which was playing on the radio.

"Come here and hand me these tools," said Finn.

"Ok," said Poppy.

"Mike and Charlie said they would help on Saturday. They're bringing some supplies and meeting us by the bridge at 7 am. Make sure you and Ella are ready. You two are in charge of food and drinks and of course you know the way. Let me do the talking. I'll let Mamo know you're hanging out with us and that we'll be back for supper."

"Got it," said Pops seriously, narrowing her eyes. She wanted to let Finn know she was dependable.

"Yeah, Mike and Charlie swore they would keep it all secret, especially when I promised them some of Mr. Timpiste's cookies as incentive," he said with a grin. "You can trust them. They're good guys."

The next day of school was half a day. Poppy was feeling so confident and happy that she actually didn't care when Gwen Grotty stuck her tongue out at her during math class. Poppy sneered at Gwen and then laughed in her face, much to Gwen's surprise. Gwen didn't know which way to look when the kids around her laughed at her. Poppy joined in with the laughter.

"Yup, it's going to be a great weekend!" she murmured.

CHAPTER 4

WHAT THEY FOUND INSIDE

Everything went as planned. By lunchtime the five of them had uncovered the little house. They sat on the pine needle floor with sunbeams scattered among them, eating sandwiches and gulping down water. They were all very tired but none of them cared because of how excited they were to finish. No one said anything for a few moments as they all gazed at the stone house with the red metal roof.

"I walked around it," said Mike, with a mouth full of peanut butter. "It's got eight sides."

"Whoa that's cool!" Charlie said adding, "It's got four windows but they're too high up to see in."

"Pass me a cookie," Mike demanded, looking at Ella.

"Don't get pushy Muggins," warned Ella, holding the cookie just out of his reach.

Mike just laughed and grabbed it from her hand. While the other four munched on cookies, Finn began walking around the perimeter of the house inspecting the beautiful stonework. He stopped and looked closely at the thick wooden arched doorway that was weathered grey and blended in with the field stone surrounding it. He pulled and pushed on the heavy black hand forged iron door handle. It didn't budge. Finn really hoped it wasn't locked. Upon closer inspection, he determined that the door was supposed to swing inward. After a few more tries, he called for Mike and Charlie to come help him push the door open. On the third push, using all their combined strength, the stubborn door slowly nudged forward with a loud creaking noise. The girls rushed to their sides and tried to peer in between the boys. They leaned into the back of Mike and Charlie and all crammed into the dimly lit cabin, gazing wide eyed at their surroundings. The room was circular, more precisely it had 8 sides like a stop sign. It was larger inside than it appeared from the outside and was open all the way to the roof. There was a large skylight overhead, presently obstructed by a sprawling tree limb. The windows were grimy and brown from years of weather and the scraping of vines. The floor was wooden and very dusty. Poppy ran her hand along the top of an enormous oak desk which seemed to almost overpower the room. Ella turned on her flashlight and the beam of light danced on a small rocking chair. It was ornately carved and on the chair seat, sat a child's tiny tin top, resting on its side. Charlie sat down on a primitive but sturdy handmade wooden chair which resided in front of an antique foot treadle sewing machine. Trying, but not succeeding to make the iron foot treadle move up and down, he decided to crawl onto the floor and give it a go with his hands. Ella strained her eyes and tried to take in the details of the room.

"This place is pretty neat," Finn said, finally breaking the silence.

"Yeah, looks like somebody lived here a long time ago." Charlie looked around the room suspiciously.

"Can't see very good in here. Does anyone see a light switch or lamp?" asked Mike.

"It's not very "*good*" said Ella, looking directly at Mike.

"What's not very good?" Mike asked looking confused.

"We can't see very "*well*" she told Mike with a huge sigh rolling her eyes.

"Are you seriously correcting…." Mike started to say but was interrupted by a shriek from Poppy.

"It's the cat!" Poppy shouted, pointing to the large orange tiger sitting on top of the desk.

"Holy moly where did *he* come from?!" bellowed Mike, backing away from the desk.

Charlie started laughing, holding onto his sides.

"That cat is HUGE! It's as big as Mr. Timpiste's cat," shouted Finn.

"You afraid of a little old cat, Mike?!" Charlie taunted. "Watch out he might attack you!"

Mike gave Charlie a ferocious look.

"Watchit Stubbs, or I'll tell the girls all about what scares you…"

"Ok Ok," laughed Charlie, holding his hands up and zipping his mouth shut.

"Why does that cat look like he's laughing at me?" complained Mike.

The cat *was* looking at Mike, shaking slightly, with a gleam in his eye. The corners of his mouth were definitely turned up.

"I'm going outside to see if I can get that tree limb off the roof. Who's going to help me?" Mike said glaring at Charlie.

The three boys left the house, leaving Poppy and Ella inside with the cat.

"He definitely was *not* here a minute ago," Poppy stated shaking her head, still surprised at how scared Mike was.

"Well he's here now," Ella answered, walking toward the cat.

"Hi Mr. Kitty," Ella crooned, reaching to pat his very large striped head. She couldn't quite reach that high and the cat seemed to lean to the left to avoid her touch.

"Well this is just the best thing ever El! We can clean this place up and have our own secret clubhouse!" Poppy said practically bursting.

"I know!" Ella squealed with delight. "We need to wash the windows and see if we can open them for some fresh air. Once we can see better we can get rid of all the dust and cobwebs."

Poppy agreed and searched around for something to stand on so she could reach the nearest window.

In the meantime, the boys were outside trying to figure out how to reach the tree limb on the roof. They worked together to drag and stack two large rocks on top of one another and then two more about a foot away. They stuck mud and leaves between the rocks to keep them from shifting. Charlie climbed on top of the first pile of rocks and Mike firmly planted his feet on the other. Clasping their hands together, Charlie and Mike hoisted Finn onto the red metal roof. Finn stretched his arms upward reaching as far as he could, while Charlie held him by the ankles and Mike kept Charlie from falling off the rocks.

"I need a few more inches!" said Finn, straining to reach the branch. Mike let go of Charlie and both he and Charlie grabbed hold of Finn's sneakers and pushed him higher.

"Got it!" shouted Finn, as he grabbed the huge branch and began to tug. It was this tug that did them all in.

First Mike crashed to the ground followed by Charlie then Finn. They landed in a pile, arms and legs sprawled in all directions and miraculously the tree limb caught on the edge of the roof, dangling precariously over their heads. Finn and Mike rolled aside and jumped up to grab the branch hanging off the side of the house, but Charlie writhed on the ground moaning and holding onto his right arm.

"Charlie you're hurt!" yelled Poppy, as the girls ran outside to see what the commotion was.

"Pull him out of the way so I can keep this branch from falling on him!" Mike shouted frantically.

Finn, Ella and Poppy carefully dragged Charlie to one side, while Mike grabbed the butt of the unruly branch dangling off the edge of the roof. With Finn's help, Mike was able to remove the tree limb and throw it onto the pile of vines.

"I think it's broken," whimpered Charlie, his face contorted with the pain.

"Oh boy," worried Ella. "I'm so sorry Charlie," she said trying to hug him.

"Get off Ella!" Mike barked sternly. "We've got to go back and get him to the doctor!"

"Ok let's go," agreed Finn.

It was a long walk back to the house and they spent the time devising a good explanation of why they were covered in dirt and scratches and how Charlie had hurt his arm.

"You're going to be the coolest kid in your class Charlie. Everyone will want to sign your cast," Ella said encouragingly, flashing her most sparkling smile at Charlie. This kindness actually conjured a smile on his smudged and tear-stained face.

"He's ok," said Finn, hanging up the phone Sunday morning after talking with Charlie. "The doctor said it's only a small fracture. He should have a cast for only about three weeks. He wants to come over but his mom won't let him. She's not too happy he climbed up that tree so high." Finn winked at Poppy. "I'm gonna call Mike and see if he wants to meet me at Charlie's. We can keep him company and watch some Star Trek."

CHAPTER 5

CLEANING HOUSE

Poppy and Ella were glad to hear that Charlie was going to be ok. After sharing a delicious Sunday brunch with Mamo, Poppy and Ella ran across the field and into the tool shed. The night before, they had packed Poppy's backpack with cleaning supplies, a few small tools and A1 oil. Grabbing a plastic bucket and the backpack from the shed, Poppy and Ella trotted across the long stretch of field that led to the bridge, very intent on the task at hand; cleaning their new clubhouse. Toby, who had been guarding the chicken house, galloped after them tail wagging and tongue hanging out, excited for the adventure as much as the girls. They filled the bucket with water from the river and walked very slowly, taking turns carrying the heavy load so the water wouldn't spill over the sides. The first glimpse of the octagonal cabin made Poppy inhale sharply and grin with delight. The day was brighter and sunnier than the one before and the red roof was the first thing that caught their eyes as they approached.

"It's really pretty in the sunlight now that we can see the whole thing," panted Ella as they approached the house.

"I'm so excited to explore the inside. It should be a lot brighter now that the skylight is clear," agreed Poppy. "I feel badly about Charlie," she said pushing open the door, plopping her backpack onto the floor and gazing up at the rooftop window.

"Me too Pops. We should try and do something nice for him this week at school. Maybe we could ask Mr. Timpiste to bake him his favorite peanut butter cookies. We could bring them to school for him."

Poppy agreed this would be the best thing to do, and then the girls unpacked their supplies. First thing they did was look for something to stand on in order to clean the grimy windows. Ella spotted a small stool that she had not noticed the day before. It was made of thick wooden logs and looked quite sturdy. They each took turns standing on the stool and washing the four windows. Ella carried it outside while Poppy grabbed the water bucket, paper towels and window cleaner. She and Poppy spent almost an hour scrubbing the grime off the window panes. The room brightened even more with the sunshine now streaming in. Ella oiled the window hinges and working together they were able to tilt them open, spilling much needed fresh air into the cabin. With the additional light from the windows, they were able to get a better look at what was inside the room. It indeed had eight field stone walls connecting to make an octagonal shape; like a stop sign. After searching more closely, they still could not find any lights or electrical outlets in the room. It didn't seem to have any electricity at all. The rocking chair occupied by the tiny toy spinning top, sat next to a little wood stove that had a long chimney which poked through the red metal roof. On the wall opposite the wood stove sat an antique foot treadle sewing machine complete with a little chair. To its left several feet away, was a small domed top trunk sitting on the floor by itself. Ella bent down and tried to open the top but it was locked.

"Look at this *ginormous* desk!" Poppy half squeaked half shouted. "It looks like it's made for a giant!" she said, opening her eyes as wide as she could.

"It does make *quite* a statement," Ella agreed, running her hands along the smooth well-worn surface.

The oversized desk was made of a rich golden colored wood with a swirling grain throughout. Poppy climbed into the bulky desk chair. Sucking in her cheeks, making her lips pucker like a fish, she widened her pretty blue eyes so she could take in the awesomeness of the giant desk that stood before her. There were cubby holes and little drawers lining the inside. Kneeling on the chair, in order to reach one of the small drawers, she pulled it open revealing a miniature muslin draw string bag filled with tiny seeds of all different colors and a small piece of paper. The paper had little holes pricked into it and didn't look like anything special. Searching through three other drawers she found more pieces of paper, all with tiny holes scattered on them.

"Ella come here and look at these papers."

Ella, who had been applying a little oil to the corners of the sewing machine treadle to make it stop squeaking, abandoned what she was doing and joined Poppy at the desk.

"What do you think of these papers El? They all have little holes in them and they all look the same."

Ella examined the papers closely.

"Hmmm strange Pops. I'm not sure what they are. Look for the key to that little trunk over there. It's locked and I'd love to see what's inside."

The two girls searched the rest of the cubby holes and felt the back of the drawers, but couldn't find anything else.

"How about those big drawers on the bottom, Pops?"

Poppy scooted onto her knees and rubbed her fingers over the lower right drawer handle, giggling as she pinched the nose and tugged the ears of a very smug looking cat face.

"This drawer handle looks like Mr. Cat!!!" Ella shouted, crouching down next to Poppy.

"You almost busted my eardrum El!" Poppy said rubbing her left ear.

"Sorry Pops but *look* at that smirk! I'd recognize it *anywhere*!" whispered Ella, trying to compensate for shouting before.

Poppy inspected the other drawers carefully. The other three pulls had a Mr. Cat on the front, each wearing a different expression. The upper right drawer handle was a happy Mr. Cat with a toothy smile.

"This one doesn't look right," Ella said pointing to the grinning cat face. "I can't picture the *real* Mr. Cat smiling."

"Look over here!" Poppy excitedly crawled over to the left side of the desk.

The lower left drawer sported a Mr. Cat with a scary hissing face. Poppy put her face close and hissed back at the angry kitty.

"This Mr. Cat is sleeping," Ella said, pointing to the top left drawer over Poppy's head. "His eyes are closed Pops."

"Whoa! I'm not surprised. Finn said that Mr. Timpiste's cat sleeps all day in the fix-it shop; doesn't even wake up when customers come in; says she only opens one eye if they scratch her head. I think…."

"Where *is* Mr. Cat anyway?!" interrupted Ella. "Have you seen him around today?"

"Nope," answered Poppy shaking her head, while stroking the ear of sleeping Mr. Cat, pulling on his chin to open the drawer. It was filled with papers and much to the girls' surprise they were covered in rows of little holes.

"This is *very* strange Ella." Scrunching up her nose as she always did when she was thinking intently, Poppy began searching each of the remaining drawers. "They're more papers in *this* drawer too! All of them are covered in holes!"

Smiling Mr. Cat's drawer held some thread, needles, a measuring tape and a pair of scissors.

"No keys," Ella said disappointedly, returning to the antique sewing machine, pumping the iron treadle with her foot until the squeak died away.

"We can try out the sewing machine though, with this stuff we found in Happy Mr. Cat's drawer." Poppy flashed an encouraging smile at Ella. She felt along the front of the desk. "There's one more drawer here. It's hard to see because it's tucked up under the front edge of the desk."

Ella was excited that Poppy had found another possible hiding place for the key. Returning to the desk, she probed the area with her fingers. She felt a long, thin curvy handle and with close inspection she saw it had a spiral pattern etched into the wood. Tracing the detail with her fingertips, she suddenly jumped backwards.

"What's the matter?" asked Poppy trying not to laugh.

"You've *got* to be kidding me," Ella said shaking her head and rolling her eyes.

"What?!" laughed Poppy looking at the drawer handle more closely.

"I've found Mr. Cat's tail!"

Poppy covered her mouth and snickered.

"That's cool!" Poppy cried as she tugged on the striped tail, but the drawer was locked.

"Oh boy," groaned Ella. "Now we're missing *two* keys!"

The girls searched the one-room house top to bottom for anything resembling a key, including a large wooden cupboard that stood on the wall opposite Mr. Cat's desk. They found nothing except for some nicely folded sewing fabric and a few bundles of sticks, probably meant to start the fire. Ella resumed cleaning and oiling the sewing mechanism of the old treadle sewing machine, while Poppy cleared the cobwebs from the tall pine cupboard.

"Look over here!" Poppy said, tugging at the corner of the large wooden cupboard. "Doesn't this look like a door hinge?"

"Yeah, it *does* look like one," Ella agreed. "Maybe there's a secret door behind the cupboard!"

"But wait… there's nothing on the outside of the cabin. Is there?"

"I don't know…. let's go look!" Ella said excitedly.

They left the little house and walked around to the back, inspecting where they thought the door might be.

"We missed this before," said Ella, pointing to a bulkhead shaped metal extension to the house.

Poppy banged on the side, scraping her knuckles on the heavy metal.

"Well, there's no entrance from *this* side," said Ella.

"That's weird. How can there be a door with nothing on the other side?" Poppy rubbed her sore knuckles.

"And what's this extension to the house for?" wondered Ella, with a sideways glance at Poppy.

"Between the missing keys and the door to nowhere, I feel like we have a lot of figuring out to do," Poppy said with a sigh.

A little discouraged, they decided to go back inside and check out the newly oiled sewing machine. It was working now. The foot treadle, which was attached to a pully, powered the sewing machine and the needle easily glided up and down, as Ella pumped with her foot. They found more sewing accessories and some thread in the drawers and agreed they would try and make a small quilt with the fabric that was in the cupboard.

Poppy stared at the old machine and thought of her mother. Her heart ached as she tried to remember the details of sitting on her mother's lap while she finished sewing Poppy a dress for Christmas. She closed her eyes and tried to recall the fragrant smell of her mother's hair, and the feeling of soft kisses on the top of her head, as her mother explained in detail how to finish the hem of her dress. Mamo had cried with Poppy and held her closely in the agonizing months that passed after her mother was gone. She could hear Mamo's words:

"Your mother will always be with you because you are made of her love, thoughts and ideas. Everything you know and love is entwined with her being. Remember her smile and the stories she told you. If you need help in times of sadness and trouble, ask her what to do and she will answer because your thoughts are mingled with hers."

56

Poppy really didn't understand all the things Mamo had whispered as she rocked her to sleep at night. But she liked to think of the words from time to time because they brought her comfort.

"Pops...Poppy...Popppppppy McGee?!!!" Ella waved her hand in front of Poppy's eyes looking concerned. "You ok?"

"Yyyeah," Poppy stammered, "just thinking...let's get going. It's almost suppertime and Mamo will be waiting for us."

CHAPTER 6

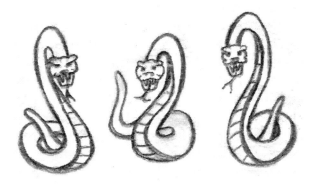

THREE LITTLE SNAKES

I t was finally the last week of school. Poppy, of course, couldn't wait for it to be over. The feeling of dread she felt each night before school had become increasingly worse. Unable to sleep, she was exhausted and trudged through the day in dire need of rest.

On Wednesday, Gwenn, Karlyn and Bonnie cornered her in the hallway between classes. They threw her books on the floor and pulled her socks down, while chanting "chatterbox, chatterbox!"

"Gonna go run and tell mommy?" sneered Gwen. "Oh wait...you don't have one," she added with a twisted smile.

"You're so mean," Poppy half whispered, as tears welled up in her eyes.

"*What* did you say you little loser? You've *always* got something to say. In fact, you *never* stop talking Chatterbox Girl!" Gwen snarled threateningly, as she pushed her pudgy forehead against Poppy's face, backing a shaking Poppy against the wall.

"Kick her!" Karlyn encouraged Gwen.

"Yeah! Get her in the shins!" chimed in Bonnie.

Gwen put all her strength into the kick that landed on Poppy's left shin. While Poppy clutched her leg and sunk to the floor in a puddle of pain and tears, the three girls took off down the hallway, laughing and looking in all directions to make sure they weren't caught. Poppy pulled herself up and hobbled to the girl's bathroom sobbing and limping as her leg throbbed with pain. She pulled her socks up as high as she could to cover the gash in her leg and the trickle of blood slithering down her ankle. She cried into a wad of scratchy school paper towels until there were no more tears left in her head.

"What do I do?" she mumbled to herself. "Now I'm late for class."

She decided to stay in the bathroom and hide out until the dismissal bell rang. Luckily it was the last class of the day and she hoped that no one would notice she was not where she was supposed to be; in class two seats behind Bonnie Craven. It was Wednesday. The day that Poppy loved to walk home with Ella. Poppy was filled with such a mixture of sadness and a longing for her home. She felt if she didn't speak she would be able to make it home and to her bedroom without falling apart. She ran to her bus and climbed into the seat that no one liked, right behind the bus driver. She pulled the hood of her sweatshirt up and buried her face in her book, *The Cricket in Times Square*. She felt herself slip into the story and become a character in the book, disappearing from her troubled world.

"I'm NOT a Chatterbox Girl. They're just wrong about that.

Two more days," she thought. *"Two more days of school and I'm free."*

Poppy ran from the bus and slipped into the front door and upstairs to her room. She climbed into bed fully clothed and wrapped herself in the blankets. She started to nod off when she was awoken by Mamo's touch.

"What's wrong with my Poppy?" Mamo said lovingly, as she stroked Poppy's damp cheek.

"I don't feel good Mamo," Poppy whispered back.

"You have a bad day at school? Ella is looking all over for you. Her mother called worried sick cause you didn't meet her after school. Miss Donahue said you didn't go to last class today either."

"I was sick in the bathroom Mamo." Poppy strained to get the words out, while her blue eyes pooled and tears streaked down her red cheeks.

"You rest right now Poppy." Mamo kissed her forehead and gently pushed back Poppy's hair. "I'll bring a snack to your room. We'll talk later about school."

As soon as Mamo left the room, Toby ran and jumped into bed with Poppy. She clamped her hands around his neck and buried her head in his fur. Toby licked all the tears from her face and she fell fast asleep feeling the true love and loyalty in Toby's heart.

Mamo was a soft-hearted woman and didn't think that making Poppy go to school the last two days was particularly important in the scheme of things. Mamo called Seamus, who was away on business, and told him that she felt Poppy could use some quiet time with her at home. Seamus always had the greatest respect for his mother, and was grateful for the love and care that she showed, by helping raise Poppy and Finn since his wife died. Seamus agreed and said that he was sure she would do what was best for Poppy. Poppy felt as if she had been released from a prison sentence and her heart almost exploded with happiness when Mamo told her she was on break from school for the summer. She reluctantly told Mamo what had happened at school, pleading with her not to tell anyone.

"It will only make it worse Mamo."

"I cannot let those girls harm you Poppy. It's not right. I will speak to the school privately. You don't need to be there."

An achy feeling started to creep into Poppy's stomach, but Mamo reassured Poppy she would "handle the little snakes." Poppy was a little unsure what Mamo meant by this comment. She suppressed a small smile when she pictured what Mamo might do to the girls, because she knew Mamo could be a tough cookie, especially when it came to defending her grandchildren. She remembered the time Mrs. McStickler had accused Finn of stealing her Halloween pumpkin from her porch. After speaking with Finn and hearing that he had nothing to do with it, Mamo had asked Mike Muggins to keep his ears peeled at school for anyone bragging about the pumpkin heist. Mike overheard Greg Grotty gloating to everyone who would listen, that he had stolen and smashed every pumpkin on Maple Street. Mike was more than happy to rat Grotty out to Mamo, who in turn reported him not to the school principal, but to

Mrs. McStickler. Poppy was sure this was much worse, since Mrs. McStickler was the school disciplinarian and assigned Greg to cafeteria duty for the next three months as punishment. Mike and Finn had reported back to Mamo that Greg looked quite smashing in his hair net and flowered apron.

So, Poppy immersed herself into helping Mamo prepare for one of her favorite events of the year; the end of school camping trip with Seamus.

CHAPTER 7

TURTLE LAKE

Each year, Seamus, Uncle Ernie, Mr. Timpiste and Miles, took Poppy, Ella and Finn on a camping and fishing trip to Turtle Lake, to celebrate the end of the school year. Finn pleaded with Seamus to let him invite Mike and Charlie along, since this year the boys weren't going to camp. Seamus agreed with the stipulation that they wouldn't torment the girls during the trip.

"I'll keep them in line Seamus," promised Finn, with a reassuring smile to his father.

The trip was an exciting tradition and they all eagerly helped load Seamus' pickup truck early

Saturday morning. After fishing rods, sleeping bags, tents and a myriad of other things were packed into Seamus' truck, Ernie arrived pulling his boat trailer with his newly acquired pickup.

Seamus, grateful for the extra room, loaded Ernie's truck with two giant coolers of prepared food that Mamo and Poppy had been getting ready for days. The coolers contained everything they needed to cook on the campfire and eat for the weekend, including some surprises mixed in for fun.

"I can't wait to see what Mamo packed for us this year!" Ella said, grinning from ear to ear.

"I helped her make everything!" Poppy proudly answered.

Mr. Timpiste and Ella's father, Miles, arrived together in the Mansfield's station wagon. Peering through the windows of the car, Charlie, Finn and Mike noticed immediately that Mr. Timpiste had a large brown box wrapped with twine in the back seat. Mike nudged Charlie and whispered that he thought it was filled with cookies. Charlie asked Mr. Timpiste if they could ride in the station wagon. He wanted to keep a close eye on the box.

"Sure! Why don't you boys climb in. It looks like we are almost ready to take off," said Mr. Timpiste.

"Cool!" shouted Mike, racing to get to the rear facing bench seat in the back of the wagon.

"Why don't you two girls ride with Uncle Ernie," Seamus said. "Miles can keep me company in my truck. We can talk over our fishing strategy on the way."

"Ok, you kids all be safe now," Mamo said, emerging from the kitchen door.

After lots of hugs and one more trip to the bathroom for Poppy, the two trucks and station wagon left the driveway with five kids hanging out of the windows, shouting goodbye.

As they bounced along in Ernie's truck, Ella thought of asking Poppy about what happened on Wednesday, or why she didn't go to school the last two days. She decided not to. She was very thoughtful in that way. She knew Poppy would probably tell her all about it during the weekend when they were alone and she was ready.

By the time they arrived at the lakefront campsite, unpacked and set up most of the tents, it was mid noon. All five kids jumped into the lake, spending a few hours doing handstands, searching for treasure on the bottom and having chicken fights; which were very entertaining for Seamus and Ernie to watch from their folding chairs on the shore. Mr. Timpiste and Miles swam out to a huge rock that was sticking at least five feet out of the lake. They stayed an hour or so talking and relaxing in the bright sunshine, looking into the clear depths for turtles. As the sun started to fall and stomachs started to rumble, it was mutually decided it was time to think about making a campfire. Charlie looked for rocks to ring the fire with, while Mike and Finn gathered dry sticks and leaves. Ella and Poppy helped Seamus set up the camping cookware and started to explore what was in the coolers. By twilight, the campfire started to crackle and soon there was a blazing fire. After a hearty dinner of Mamo's pre-packed hamburgers, hot dogs and corn on the cob wrapped in tin foil grilled over the fire, the kids eagerly awaited one of their favorite parts of the trip; Mr. Timpiste's stories. He had been in the military, and after had a career piloting people and goods in and out of Alaska. Many a pilot had lost their life doing just as Mr. Timpiste had; flying through mostly uncharted freezing territory, often during stormy weather and white out conditions. But Mr. Timpiste had proven to be a very skilled pilot indeed. They gathered around the fire and listened as Mr. Timpiste told his story:

"I got a radio call one night from Cub's Cove, one of the most remote villages I had ever flown to. A little girl's appendix had burst and she was in a terrible way. I had to get to her as quickly as I could, to save her life. I had no trouble getting to her, but on the way

back it started snowing harder than you could imagine. The menacing flakes were driving down fast and thick, pounding against the wings of the plane and visibility was now at a minimum. My heart raced. If the temperature dropped even further, the snow would turn to ice and that would mean trouble. The wind howled and moaned, tossing my airplane around like a toy. I could barely swallow and my head reeled with the thought of going down. I had no choice but to keep heading in the direction of the nearest hospital and hope for the best. I never concentrated so much in my life. The little girl cried the whole ride but her mother was silent as stone. The hospital was equipped with high powered beacon lights just for the purpose of guiding planes in. I think it was a mixture of determination and a whole lot of luck that allowed me to hit my target. The incredible surge of relief I felt when I saw those lights was a feeling I'll never forget. I was lucky enough to see them blinking in the distance and I landed the plane, scraping the belly of it on the ice and snow that had already piled up. I don't think I'll ever forget the look on the mother's face when she grabbed my hand and gazed at me with wild appreciative eyes before we entered the hospital doors."

Other than the crackling of the fire and the noise of the katydids, all was silent at the campfire, as Mr. Timpiste told his tale. Poppy leaned forward, her eyes round and wide.

"Whoa," said Mike, very impressed with Mr. Timpiste's story.

Charlie could only shake his head in disbelief because his mouth was filled with Mr. Timpiste's peanut butter cookies.

"What happened to the little girl?" asked Ella leaning forward in anticipation.

"Well…. the very next spring, she invited me to her parent's family bakery to sample some of her own homemade oatmeal cookies. They were so tasty, that I asked her to show me how to make them and she

shared her secret recipe with me. I became a regular at the bakery each time I was in the area. When I would visit, she would show me a new recipe and we would cook up a batch if I had the time. That was the beginning of my cookie baking career. I saved all her recipes and well…. you're eating her peanut butter cookies as we speak."

Mr. Timpiste pointed to Charlie as he stuffed yet another cookie in his mouth. Everyone laughed at the sight of Charlie who had gone red in the face; cheeks puffed out, munching and looking a little embarrassed.

"By the time she was old enough to marry, Evangeline, that was her name, though everyone called her Evie, had lost her father. He was a very good man. He took care of his family and worked long hours at the bakery. Well anyway, she asked me to walk her down the aisle at her wedding….and that's what I did. It was one of the proudest days of my life."

Mr. Timpiste's eyes were looking a little glossy in the firelight. Ernie and Seamus, who had heard many of Mr. Timpiste's stories throughout the years, suddenly appeared out of the darkness. They had just finished assembling the largest of the three tents that the men would share.

"Time to hit the hay," Seamus announced, while helping a very sleepy Poppy to her feet.

"Early morning tomorrow," added Ernie. "The fish will be searching for breakfast."

"I'll walk you girls to your tent," said Miles.

Poppy was asleep seconds after her head hit the pillow while Ella silently listened to the crickets, closing her eyes and playing a movie in her head. She pictured the freezing cold night and the snow pounding on the wings of the plane and imagined how scared Evie must have been. Just before she fell asleep, Ella decided for certain, that Mr. Timpiste was a true hero.

The next morning, Poppy was abruptly awakened by a very large object that came crashing through the side of her tent.

"You're crushing me!" screamed Ella. Poppy had suddenly steam rolled her.

Both Poppy and Ella grabbed at the tent flaps trying to escape from the tangled mess inside.

"What do you think you're doing Stubbs?!" Ella yelled at poor Charlie, who was trying to recover from crashing into the tent. Meanwhile, Mike was hysterically laughing.

"He pushed me!" Charlie defended himself, turning on Mike and chasing him down to the lake.

"You run like a girl!" Finn shouted to Charlie.

"And what's *that* supposed to mean?" Ella glared at Finn.

Finn, who knew better than to get Ella riled up and in a debate about boys vs. girls, decided to change the subject very quickly.

"Your hair is in a knot," Finn teased, poking Ella in the side and immediately taking off in the direction of Mike and Charlie.

"Boys," grumbled Ella rolling her eyes.

Seamus, Miles, Ernie and Mr. Timpiste, who were already eating scrambled eggs by the fire, were thoroughly enjoying the side show.

"Eggs are ready!" Seamus announced still laughing.

The plan for the day was to fish in the morning and then take a hike up Wesson Hill in the afternoon. Charlie started off the day by falling into the lake fully clothed. Thankfully he had just had his cast removed on the last day of school. Of course, Finn and Mike were hysterically laughing.

"You two are the worst!" said Ella, scowling at Mike and Finn. "Poor Charlie……"

"Poor Charlie," mimicked Mike sarcastically.

"Oh boy, Mike…. I wouldn't go there," Finn said, not laughing anymore.

The sun's rays sparkled on the surface of Turtle Lake and a light warm breeze rocked Ernie's fishing boat on the water. Ella and Finn caught the most fish. Mike and Charlie spent most of their time fooling around and trying to push each other off the boat. Poppy's fish enjoyed a morning snack, as she daydreamed about the octagonal cabin in the woods. She wondered about the hidden door behind the cupboard and what it must lead to. She decided to wait until later in the day, when the grownups weren't around, to ask Finn and the boys for their help to move the cupboard.

The afternoon hike up Wesson Hill was very steep. Mike and Charlie charged ahead full speed while Finn hung back with Ella and Poppy. Grabbing at one last tree and hoisting herself up to the top ledge, Poppy crashed onto the ground panting.

"Look at that view!" Ella said breathlessly.

"I can see for miles!" Finn shaded his eyes searching for any landmarks he might know.

"I'm too tired to look," Poppy mumbled, as she rolled over onto her side.

Miles helped Poppy to her feet and handed her his binoculars.

"Take a look."

She adjusted the lens and after searching for something interesting, she saw a red-tailed hawk sitting in a distant tree.

"Let me look Pops," said Finn holding out his hands.

While Finn searched the landscape for "more cool animals," Poppy and Ella sat down in the tall green grass peppered with wildflowers. Poppy gazed out over the miles of landscape below and let out a huge sigh.

"I don't ever want to go back to school," she said quietly to Ella, a look of dismay on her face.

"You still haven't told me what happened, Pops."

"I didn't want to talk about it---just wanted it to go away."

Poppy told Ella what had happened at school, showing her the now scabbed-over gash in her leg.

"They called me a Chatterbox Girl," mumbled Poppy with a frown.

"They're toast!" Finn said angrily, overhearing what Poppy had said.

"Who has toast?" Charlie asked running over to the girls.

"That loser, Gwen Grotty, kicked Poppy on the leg! Game's over, Pops; Charlie, Mike and I are gonna make their life a misery next year!" vowed Finn.

This brought a smile to Poppy's face.

"Well, Mamo already told me she was going to take care of it. She even called them little snakes!"

This made everyone laugh because they all knew Mamo was a good person to have on your side.

Following a grilled fish dinner, the kids roasted marshmallows around the campfire while Seamus and the guys hung out by their tent swapping stories, sneaking a beer while the kids were busy.

"So, you think it's a door hinge?" Finn asked, sounding excited at the idea of a secret door.

"Maybe there's a skeleton behind the door!" Mike added.

"Don't be ridiculous!" Ella scolded Mike, secretly hoping there was nothing remotely like a skeleton on the other side of the door.

"We're your movers!" said Charlie proudly flexing his muscles.

Poppy had trouble falling asleep in her tent that night. Her mind kept racing with ideas of what could be behind the door, and trying to figure out where it could lead to, especially since there was nothing on the other side of the wall.

CHAPTER 8

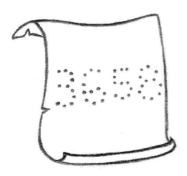

PINHOLES AND KEYHOLES

S unlight poured into the kitchen window and a soft breeze slipped through the back-screen door, gently rocking the handwoven baskets lining the heavy beamed ceiling in the McGee kitchen. The smell of Mamo's homemade cinnamon raisin bread fresh from the oven, mixed with bacon, eggs and freshly grilled hash browns, was incentive for the tired campers to roll out of bed. Poppy chattered away, informing Mamo of pretty much everything that happened that weekend. Mamo was a good listener and commented only when Poppy stopped to take a breath. Ella and Finn were content to eat their breakfast and occasionally gave each other a sideways glance when Poppy's stories became a little embellished.

"Well it sounds like you had a wonderful time," Mamo was able to sneak in when Poppy paused to take a bite of toast.

"We sure did!" answered Seamus, suddenly appearing in the kitchen. "I am one lucky man to wake up to a breakfast like this!"

"Morning Seamus!" Finn and Ella said at the same time.

Poppy jumped up and hugged her father around the waist.

"Love you Seamus."

"Love you too Pops," he answered, with a kiss on top of her head.

"Mike and Charlie are coming over later. Do you mind if we set up a couple of the tents by the river? We were gonna do some fishing for craw dads – maybe build a small dam to catch them, and then camp out for the night?" Finn asked his father.

"Finn said that Ella and I could help out!" added Poppy hopefully.

"Sounds like fun. I wish I could join you but I plan to spend the day re-shingling the last side of the barn. Ernie's coming over to give me a hand. It's ok with me, if you bring Toby and keep an eye on the girls."

It was Mamo's turn to sit and have breakfast while Seamus and the kids cleaned the kitchen and put everything back in its place. As usual, dish washing ended with Finn towel snapping Ella and Poppy until Mamo shooed them out the door.

"Yup, it's a door hinge," said Finn, stretching to peer around the side of the cupboard. "Charlie, Mike, give me a hand."

Finn pulled from one side while Charlie and Mike pushed from the other. The cupboard moved only a few inches, creaking and scraping the floor.

"This thing is heavy!" Mike said panting and wiping his forehead.

"Let us help!" Ella forced her way between Mike and Charlie, bracing her hip against the side. "Poppy, you pull with Finn from the other side."

With all their combined strength, they were able to slowly edge the cupboard aside exposing a wooden door. Toby, who had been watching from underneath the desk, suddenly became very interested in the newly exposed entrance. He trotted over and began sniffing the floor, scratching at the door and barking.

"This is awesome!" said Finn, a little out of breath as he grabbed the door handle. He turned and pulled but nothing happened.

"Great…. it's locked," moaned Ella. "Now we're missing *three* keys!"

"What do you mean three keys?" Finn asked Ella.

Ella first showed them the little locked dome topped trunk. Then she pointed out the cat faced drawers and the locked drawer with the cat tail handle.

"That's a freaky desk," Mike made a disgusted face.

"Dude, what's your problem with cats?" Charlie punched Mike in the arm, which immediately prompted a wrestling match.

"There's no key hole," Finn said, as he crouched by the newly exposed door handle.

"How do you unlock a door with no key hole?" Charlie asked, sneaking one more poke in Mike's side.

"I don't know," Finn shook his head frustrated. "You girls are gonna have to figure this out. We need to go back to the field and finish setting up the tents. I'll leave Toby behind to keep you company."

Ella and Poppy had searched everywhere they could think the missing keys might be. They were truly stumped. Toby camped out in front of the door still sniffing the knob and trying to pry it open with his paws. Poppy hooked her left arm around Toby's neck and kneeled on the floor to inspect the door knob closely.

"What do you think Toby?" she asked, rubbing her cheek against his.

She ran her finger along the top of the little brass balls that circled the door handle and was very excited when one suddenly popped inward, making a loud clicking noise. Each time she pushed one of the balls, the previous one popped out. The girls were very excited about the new discovery but were not quite sure what to do next.

"This is sooooo frustrating!" Poppy said with a big sigh.

"What do we have to work with Pops?"

Before Poppy could answer, Ella answered her own question.

"We have a stack of papers with pin holes in them and a tiny bag of seeds. That's all we have." Ella pulled the papers out of the desk drawers and one by one held them up to the light of the window. The last piece she inspected was the smallest piece of paper which came from the cubby hole in the back of the desk. "Look at this!" Ella shouted. The numbers three, six, five, eight were clearly outlined with tiny pin holes.

"Maybe it's a code!" Poppy said enthusiastically, racing over to the door. She tried pushing in the buttons one at a time, but Poppy wasn't sure which one to start with.

"Make believe it's a clock," suggested Ella. "*One* should be just to the right of the top button."

Poppy placed her index finger on the little brass balls. Starting at the top center ball, she counted clockwise; *one, two, three*. She pushed the ball in, it clicked. Then she went forward, *four, five, six,* she again pushed the ball in and heard a second click. She went back one ball to *five,* pushed it in and once again heard a clicking sound. Finally, she counted forward three balls, *six, seven, eight,* pushed in and heard a loud *clack*. She stood and turned the door handle and pulled. The door slowly creaked open exposing eight steps down into blackness.

CHAPTER 9

ECHOES IN THE DARK

Toby bolted down the stairs and disappeared into the darkness.

"We did it!!!" Ella and Poppy both screamed, clutching hands and jumping up and down. Ella followed first, creeping cautiously down the first few stairs. Poppy, who was afraid of the dark, planted her feet, hesitant to follow Ella.

"TOBYYYY!" yelled Ella.

"Toby, Toby, Toby!"

An eerie echo emerged from the darkness. Poppy's eyes widened and she backed away from the door. Ella turned and scrambled up the stairs.

Poppy wanted to slam the door closed, but she wanted Toby back even more.

"Toby!" both girls shouted together, leaning toward the gaping darkness below.

The border collie burst out of the inky darkness and bolted up the stairs, tongue hanging out of his mouth, tail wagging excitedly, jumping and circling the girls.

"I guess Toby's ok with whatever is down there." Poppy looked at Ella blinking slowly, sucking in her breath. "Let's go get Finn."

All five of them, plus an over excited Toby, returned with flashlights and lanterns they had borrowed from the barn. Ella had excitedly told the boys about the papers with the pin holes and how they had solved the mystery of the lock.

"I figured out that the buttons push in!" Poppy said breathlessly, as they ran through the dark field on their way back to the cabin.

Ella and Poppy were very happy with how amazed the boys were, with their success. Poppy was especially glad when she did anything that impressed Finn, while Ella just liked showing up the boys any chance she could get. As soon as they opened the door to the cabin, Toby bolted across the room and disappeared down the stairway.

"With an echo like that, it sounds like a tunnel," Finn said peering down the stairway, shouting

"Helloooooo!? Toby seems to think it's safe. I'll go in first and check it out," he said bravely.

"We're right behind you," answered Mike.

"We are?" Charlie asked with a concerned look on his face, but then with a quick glance at the girls he added, "Yeah I got your back."

Poppy and Ella waited just a few minutes, but then couldn't stand the suspense. They edged their way forward into the tunnel, that was aglow with light from the boys' lanterns.

"Wait for us! Wait for us! Wait for us!" shouted Poppy, her voice echoing off the walls of the tunnel.

Toby sideswiped Finn and screeched to a halt at Ella's side.

"This is mega cool!" Charlie admired his surroundings, turning in circles holding his lantern high in the air.

"Let's see where it leads!" Mike whispered loudly. "I think we shouldn't shout anymore. Who knows what's down here."

"Ok now your freaking me out," Poppy blurted out as she linked arms with Finn.

Charlie raised his arm, shining the lantern light in his face. "I'm gooooooing to eeeeat you aliiiiive!" Charlie teased Poppy in his scariest monster voice.

Poppy screamed so shrilly that everyone had to cover their ears until the echoes of her scream and Toby's barking faded away.

"Ok, knock it off Charlie!" Finn said sternly. "Let's keep going."

They followed the tunnel until they came to a set of stairs that led upward. At the top of the stairs was another doorway. Luckily, this time the door was unlocked and swung inward with a creak. They all crammed into the room.

"It's an office," whispered Ella.

"Yeah, and no one has been here in a really long time. Look at all the cobwebs," Charlie said, waving his arms around trying to clear them away.

"There's another door over here." Mike crossed the room. He nervously turned the knob and peered inside, trying to see in the dim light. His heart was pounding, but he didn't want to let on that he was scared. Holding his lantern in the air he edged forward.

"What's all this stuff?" Charlie pushed his way past Mike. "It looks like some sort of factory."

"It's not a factory. It's a grist mill!" said Ella, shining her flashlight at a huge round stone set on its side. "See, here's the mill stone. I've read about them in school! The local farmers used to bring their grain to the mill and have it ground into flour."

"Oooooh yeah!" Poppy said a little less worried now. I've read about a mill like this in one of my books! It probably has a big wheel outside that powers the whole place!"

"Look! There's a window over here. Shine your flashlights outside so we can see!" Finn said, as he peered into the darkness.

"It's too dark to really see anything. Let's come back tomorrow in the daylight, so we can check this place out," Ella suggested.

Finn and Mike didn't want to leave just yet, but they were tired and reluctantly agreed it might be a good idea to head back.

"Ok Toby, lead the way home," Finn told the dog.

They climbed down the set of stairs and back through the tunnel, up the second set of stairs and into the cabin. They started their trek through the dark woods. Poppy and Ella were on either side of Finn, their arms linked with his. Neither girl wanted to admit they were frightened of the night woods. The walk back was difficult in the dark. Charlie tripped on a tree root and fell flat on the ground. Mike hoisted him up and walked next to him shining the light ahead, mumbling that one broken arm a year was enough. By the time they made it back to the tents they were all exhausted. Finn, Charlie and Mike crammed into the larger tent while Poppy, Ella and Toby crawled into the other. With both girls' arms wrapped around him, Toby fell half asleep, with one ear propped up and the other slightly drooping. He was after all, on guard duty.

CHAPTER 10

TIME STANDS STILL AT THE MILL

T he breakfast table was very busy the next morning. Mike, Charlie, Finn, Ella and Poppy chowed down, practically stuffing the food in their mouths and no one was talking.

"My goodness you kids are quiet this morning!" Mamo said a little suspiciously.

"We're super hungry Mamo," Finn said in a muffled voice, his mouth stuffed with toast. "Yeah thanks Mamo," Charlie added, after swallowing his milk.

"Uh-huh, well you coming back for lunch, or you want me to pack a picnic basket for the day?"

"Picnic basket!" said Poppy and Mike together.

"You have big plans today?"

"Yes! We're working on building a dam in the river so we can catch some crawdads," Finn answered his grandmother while giving a warning look to the other kids.

They all worked together, clearing the breakfast table and washing the dishes. By the time they had finished, Mamo had packed a wonderful lunch for them including sandwiches, chips, apples and some sodas that Ernie had dropped off the night before.

The first one back to the cabin was Toby. He raced ahead and circled back over and again, barking and wagging his tail at top speed, encouraging the kids to keep up. It was Poppy's turn to trip on a tree root and she landed on her stomach, belly flop style. Finn and Charlie had her back up on her feet before she could even react, and they were off again. Ella pushed the heavy door open. Toby disappeared down the tunnel stairs. The boys piled into the room followed by Poppy, who was still a little winded from her fall. The tunnel seemed less ominous during the daytime and the second time around.

"Hey there's a lamp up here," Ella said, pointing her flashlight up on the tunnel wall, illuminating an antique oil lamp.

Finn fished around in his backpack. His fingers finally wrapped around the book of matches he had stashed inside. Glancing at Charlie first, Finn asked Mike to give him a boost with ten fingers. Leaning against the tunnel wall, one foot supported by Mike, he struck a match and was surprised when the wick reluctantly ignited. The flickering flame lit up the tunnel.

"There's another one over here!" Poppy pointed excitedly to the opposite wall at the other end.

"The walls are made of brick." Charlie slid his palms along the rough surface.

Poppy walked back and forth, feeling the roughness of the bricks, taking in the smells and hollow sounds of their voices in the long-forgotten tunnel.

"This one looks loose and it's sticking out!" Poppy said tugging on a brick jutting out further than the others.

"Don't do that Poppy!" shouted Finn, his words echoing through the air. "We don't know...."

Poppy was already holding the loosened brick in her left hand while probing the empty hole it left with her other.

"Little pieces of..."

"Look! They're little wooden animals!" Ella said excitedly, shining her light on the pieces of wood Poppy displayed in her outstretched hands.

"There's a pig, a cow and a giraffe!"

Toby barked at the office door at the end of the tunnel, while they all crowded around Poppy, peering at the little hand carved animals.

"Pretty cool Pops," Finn said roughing up her hair.

Poppy carefully placed the little animals back in their hiding place and replaced the brick.

"I'm gonna keep them in their brick house for now," she grinned, feeling very proud of her discovery.

At Toby's urging, they ran to the stairs that led up to the office they had explored the night before. The warm summer sun's light strained to shine through the grimy windows of the room, resulting in golden dust filled beams that dimly lit the office. The resulting atmosphere in the room was museum like. An antique desk was adorned with a quill pen and ink bottle. Ella blew a layer of dust from the top of a ledger and gingerly opened the book which contained detailed sales accounts penned in a large scrawling hand. Poppy carefully cranked the handle of a tiny Victrola record player, a miniature version of the one in Seamus' office. Pushing the tiny brass lever to the on position, she placed the needle on the edge of the thick antique black disc. The lyrics of "You Are My Sunshine" filled the room with a beautiful eerie melody. Ella and Poppy glided around the room, their arms held high, gracefully flapping like birds in slow motion, quietly giggling and smiling from ear to ear, longing for this magical moment to go on forever. The thumping of the needle against the label in the center of the old 78 rpm record and a shout from the next room snapped the girls back to reality. Poppy replaced the needle, shut off the mechanism and closed the lid. Seamus had shown her the proper way to preserve such a wonderful treasured item.

"This place is beyond cool!" Mike's eyes were wide as he swept his gaze over the wooden gears, pullies and shafts.

"Look at the size of these grinding stones!" Ella added, stroking the smooth tremendous circular stones.

"It's like being inside one of Mr. Timpiste's antique clocks!" Finn agreed. His heart was racing with excitement as his mind expanded and absorbed the wonder of this phenomenal place. "Look at this giant clock on the wall. I bet it hasn't run for years!"

"I can see the huge waterwheel outside!" Charlie shouted peering out of the window.

He dashed toward the door on the other side of the room. It led to a set of stairs that sunk into a grassy embankment. Circling around and down toward the river, Charlie and Mike followed by Finn and Ella, made their way to the other side of the grist mill. The river around the wheel was quite low in this part and the wheel itself remained quiet and still. Poppy, who had stayed behind in the mill office, to look through the collection of antique 78 rpm records she had found in the Victrola cabinet, suddenly flew down the stairs holding both hands in the air.

"Look what I found! Look what I found!" she shouted over the noise of the river.

They all crowded around her as she held out her palms. In each of Poppy's hands were long, thin, ornate skeleton keys embellished at the tops with tiny Mr. Cat faces.

CHAPTER 11

A CHATTERBOX & CHEATERS

P oppy grinned at Ella and shook with excitement.

"Holy moly Poppy! *where* did you find those keys?!" shouted Ella, staring at her friend.

Poppy squealed and laughed and danced in circles around Ella and the boys.

"Oooook she's lost it," said Mike rolling his eyes.

Everyone burst out laughing, including Poppy.

"Well, these must be the right keys!" Finn said excitedly. They each have Mr. Cat heads on them!"

"Yeah, watch out Mike, don't touch 'em. You might get bitten," Charlie snickered.

"You're a real comedian Stubbs," Mike smirked at Charlie.

"You still haven't answered me Pops. Where'd you find them?" Ella asked, her eyes wide with anticipation.

"Well, I opened the bottom of the Victrola cabinet to see what other records were there. I found one of Seamus' favorites; 'Jeepers Creepers' by Satchmo…. you know…. Louis Armstrong…. I put it on and it sounded so great! But then something happened to the needle and it started sounding all fuzzy….so I…."

"Yes, yes, but what does *that* have to do with the keys?!" Ella interrupted.

"I'm getting there," Poppy said.

"Well you're taking a *million* years!" said Mike impatiently.

"Don't interrupt Muggins! I was…."

"Ok, ok, Pops…never mind that. The keys…*where* did you find the keys?" asked Finn, trying to get Poppy back on track.

Poppy sighed deeply and continued.

"Well there's a little drawer in the front of the cabinet and I looked in there for a new needle. I found a little tin box with some needles *and* THESE KEYS WERE IN THERE TOO!!!"

"It's lucky you like music so much Pops, or you might never have found them." Finn smiled at his sister.

"I can't wait another second!" Ella tugged on Poppy's overall strap pulling her back toward the door to the mill. "Let's go see if they work!"

"You guys coming?" Poppy yelled, craning her neck to look back at the boys, while Ella, who now had them at a slow run, increased her pace even more.

The boys quickly decided they'd rather hang out at the grist mill to work on getting the water wheel turning again.

"We'll catch up with you later!" shouted Finn, as Ella pulled Poppy through the door and out of sight.

"Jeepers creepers I'm *soooo* excited!"

"Wait!" Poppy cried, "I want to stop and get the little wooden animals!"

Ella abruptly stopped and Poppy smashed into the back of her. Luckily the flames were still burning on the wall lamps, and Ella held the flashlight for extra light while Poppy searched the wall for the loosened brick.

"It was much easier to find the first time," Poppy mumbled, feeling along the wall.

"It was just luck that you did!" Ella agreed. "I guess I'll leave them here for now. They're safe in their little brick house. The suspense is killing me! Let's go!" shouted Poppy. "I can't wait to see what's in the desk and the little trunk! I hope these are the right keys!"

"Me too!" Ella chased Poppy through the tunnel and up the stairs into the cabin. "Open the desk drawer first!"

"Here, you do it El," Poppy handed her both keys.

Ella chose the longer of the two keys. She grasped Mr. Cat's face which had its eyes closed as if sleeping, and slid it into the little keyhole that was almost totally obscured by the cat tail handle. She tried turning to the left and then the right. There was a soft clicking noise. Both girls held their breath while Ella pulled on Mr. Cat's tail. The drawer slid open noiselessly. A single item lay listlessly on its side. Both girls stared and exhaled slowly. Poppy reached in and pulled out a very old pair of brass, wire rimmed glasses. They seemed extremely fragile. Two bottle thick glass ovals were held together with a band of gold. Each side had a thin brass wire that ended with a curly C shape, which Poppy looped behind her ears.

"I can't see *anything* with these glasses on! *Everything* is blurry."

"Let me try Pops!"

Poppy unhooked the wires from her ears and gently handed the spectacles to Ella.

"Whoa! You're not kidding!" Ella gazed around the room holding her hands out in front of her dramatically. "Well I hope whatever is in the tiny trunk is a little more exciting."

Poppy sat on the floor with her legs crossed in front of the tiny dome topped box. Ella joined her, a little disappointed with their discovery.

"Here, can you keep them in your pocket?" Ella slid the tiny glasses into the front bib pocket of Poppy's overalls.

This time Poppy placed the smaller key, topped with Mr. Cat's smiling face, into the lock on the trunk. With a click and a quick lift of the lid, Ella and Poppy crammed their faces together to peer inside.

"What *is* that?" Ella wondered half aloud.

Poppy reached down gently, slipping her fingers around an exquisite but very symmetrically shaped item, about the size of a melon. She held it gingerly in her hands, at eye level, between herself and Ella. It seemed as if a soft glow emitted from the sleek sides that were adorned with images and bedazzled with twinkling pins of light, that came from within. Poppy lowered her hands and the triangular like shape opened and morphed into four smaller pyramid shapes.

"Wait a minute!" said Ella, eyes wide, "It's a cootie catcher!"

"A fortune teller!" Poppy shook her head in agreement.

"Just like Angie Acushla's from school!" they both said together.

"How does it even work?" Poppy asked skeptically.

"She usually has a waiting list of girls in the playground. She spells out your first name, asks you a color and a number and then opens one of the flaps inside and it tells you which boy in the class you're in love with."

"Oh yeah, well *that* seems pretty accurate," said Poppy rolling her eyes.

"I think Finn's name is under *all* the secret flaps." Ella's comment made both girls shake with laughter. "This one is definitely *not* made of paper."

"Yeah, it feels smooth like one of your mom's pretty dangle bracelets," Poppy agreed. "Look at all the pictures…there's an owl and a…"

"Cheetah…that's a cheetah right there…see his spots?" Ella pointed to the sleek feline. "And it's wearing glasses!"

Both girls giggled.

"Where's the light coming from?"

"It's not really a light. It's more of a glow," Ella observed rotating it in her hands.

"Oh, what a surprise," she said sarcastically, holding it up for Poppy to inspect, "and *there's* Mr. Cat!"

"He's on the cootie catcher too?!" Poppy' eyes widened and she shook her head. "That cat seems to *own* this joint!"

"There's no words or flaps though." Ella looked concerned. She tried moving the cootie catcher in and out, just like she had seen Angie Acushla do in the playground at school. Nothing happened, just a soft eerie clicking noise as the little pyramids met and then separated. She almost dropped the cootie catcher because of its size and slippery surface.

"Here, let me help you," Poppy said smiling at her friend.

Poppy took one side and Ella the other. Their fingers pushed and pulled the underside of the cootie catcher. Little bursts of light shot from its depths into the air. The room appeared to darken. All either girl could see, was the other's face in the glow of ever growing light and a spectrum of color swirling and hovering all around them. It all happened so suddenly that neither girl had any time to react. In the blink of an eye, the girls were no longer sitting on the floor of the octagonal cabin. They were somewhere new; somewhere unlike anywhere they had gone before. A place with a landscape more like the worlds described in Poppy's books, than in the world in which they lived.

CHAPTER 12

CHEETAH CHEATERS

A warm breeze, slipping through a field of slender light green daisy stems, danced across the girls' eyelids, which they were both surprised they had closed. Poppy's blue eyes mirrored Ella's brown eyes for a split second, before they took in their surroundings. They were sitting crossed legged opposite one another, just as before, but now surrounded by a million daisies swaying back and forth in the breeze.

"Are we dreaming?" Ella whispered to Poppy. Before Poppy could answer, their attention was drawn to something approaching them, parting the tops of the flowers as it came closer.

"Well I see you finally made it," Mr. Cat said, as he poked his large, furry, orange striped head through the stems.

He sat between the two flabbergasted friends, winding his long, striped tail around his paws, peering from Ella to Poppy and then back to Ella again.

"Cat got your tongue?" Mr. Cat laughed, his body shaking as he was obviously cracking himself up.

"Mansfield, McGee, snap out of it!" he abruptly said a little louder.

"How do you know my last name?" was all Ella could think to say.

Poppy simply blinked.

"Well, we met over a month ago," Mr. Cat looked a little confused.

"Can I pat you?!" Poppy burst out loudly.

"I'm not really into that kind of thing," Mr. Cat answered, scrunching up the left side of his face.

"Where are we? Why can you talk? Where did the cabin go? Is this a dream? Mr. Cat, why...."

"Whoa, *slooooow* down Chatterbox Girl," Mr. Cat interrupted, holding up one paw in front of Poppy. "*First* of all, the name is James.... Mr. Cat is a little too formal for my taste," he said with a slight smirk.

"Wait...*what* did you call me?!" Poppy said a bit angrily.

"Simmer down McGee," Mr. Cat said with a chuckle. "I called you a Chatterbox Girl because what *you* have been referring to as a cootie catcher is *actually* called a chatterbox in this world. You're the one *meant* to find the chatterbox. It works only for those who are destined to carry on the story. It's been called many things throughout the years and in many places; chatterbox, salt cellar, whirlybird, fortune teller, cootie catcher. But *yours* is the only magical one in the world."

"*Oooooooh*, I see. It's just some of the kids at school...."

"What story?" Ella asked, interrupting Poppy.

"The *story* is the essence of this world. The reason I led you to the octagonal cabin. It's why I am speaking with you now, and as it unravels, it shows us what is to come."

"You're a really smart cat," Poppy said peering into his amber eyes.

"Why thank you, Miss McGee."

"You can call me Poppy," she said with a huge grin, resisting the urge to stroke his sizeable furry striped cheeks.

The girls rose from the soft bed of daisies and accompanied James the cat through the bowing stems, to a cliff that rimmed the edge of the sea of white flowers. The fragrances and beauty of this new place completely enveloped their senses. The sky was a brilliant wash of blue, garnished with wispy clouds in shades of pomegranate and periwinkle, illuminated by a vivid glowing sun. Transparent rainbow tinted dragonflies plummeted and pounced, diving and rising up again with the light breeze.

"This place is beautiful!"

"I think so too Ella," answered James the cat. "It's fashioned from the minds of those who have visited in the past and those who are here in the present. The imaginations of the Chatterbox travelers, mixed with their hopes and dreams as well as their fears and disappointments, blend together to form the anatomy of this ever-changing world. Nothing stays the same for very long. The present and future of its existence are being shaped as we speak."

Poppy and Ella peered over the edge of the cliff. It appeared they were standing at the precipice of a very tall cone shaped mountain. They could just make out a well-worn red clay dirt path, winding around the rim of the mountain. The path disappeared as it seemingly entered the rock face and then reappeared further below. In the distance they could see three other cone shaped mountain peaks, their tiny points rising up to mingle among the clouds. Snaking its way through the valleys below was a wide river with fields of green on either side.

"Whoa, we're at the top of one of those mountains!" Poppy shouted, pointing at the beautiful landscape.

"This world looks like a giant chatterbox...with its four peaks," Ella marveled."

"Where do we go from here?" Poppy asked, searching around her feet for James the cat.

James was thoroughly enjoying a good scratch against a scraggly old log, but he suddenly turned tail and trotted toward a cluster of old elm trees at the edge of the daisy field.

"Follow me," he said to the girls.

"Hmmm, here we go again, following a cat into an unknown forest," thought Ella out loud.

As soon as they passed by the first few towering trees, they found themselves on a simple path that wound its way further into the woods. The trail had a very different atmosphere than the dazzling field of daisies. It was cooler. The canopy formed by the ancient timber blocked out most of the sun. The earth under their feet was a rich dark red and the air smelled of pine and cedar. Poppy breathed deeply.

"This forest smells like Mamo's cedar hope chest where she stores all the quilts she's made."

Ella agreed. On cold snowy nights both girls loved curling up on the couch, under Mamo's blankets in front of the fire, watching their favorite shows on television. Poppy's favorite quilt was made from Seamus' old flannel work shirts, while Ella's was the one stitched from Mamo's well-worn dresses.

The tinkling of wind chimes and a clattering noise from somewhere in the woods caught their attention, but neither Poppy nor Ella could tell exactly where the sound was coming from. The trees were enormous in size, larger than either girl had seen before. They had lost sight of James, but kept following the trail until they spotted an enormous oak tree. Poppy and Ella pressed against the tree, one girl on either side, trying and failing to reach each other's hands.

"We would need at least three more people to connect our hands." Ella peered up at the towering giant.

"Are you two tree huggers coming or not?" James asked from somewhere ahead.

They scrambled back onto the path and through some low blueberry bushes that were filled with delicious looking berries.

"This reminds me.... I'm starving." Poppy pulled some blueberries off the bush and started munching away.

"Yummm, these are so good," said Ella with her mouth full of berries.

They spent more than a few minutes gobbling down the sweet blue snacks, while James waited impatiently nearby. The air was filled with tiny sounds, both on the forest floor and high above in the canopy. Chirping, tapping, rustling and scratching composed the audible background in the woodland symphony, but the forest became still, and the noises abruptly ceased as a low chirping sound escalated, becoming louder and more powerful. Poppy and Ella turned their attention to the source of the sound expecting to see a large bird, but were quite surprised at what they laid their eyes upon. Poppy grabbed Ella's hand and squeezed. The two girls planted their feet firmly in the soil, their wide eyes locked upon the top of a large boulder about 20 feet away. A magnificent and powerful looking cheetah sat majestically atop the boulder. Its curvy muscular shoulders poised, its large bewhiskered face staring straight at them. Her coat was smooth and spotted. A shrill chirping noise that cheetahs are famous for, emitted from her savage looking mouth.

"Hey Firinne!"

"O hey James!"

Ella and Poppy stood very still, their fingers and lips stained blue from the berries, shocked at the sight of a real live ferocious cheetah, but even more surprised that she and James had just exchanged salutations.

"Miss Mansfield, Miss McGee this is my dear friend Firinne," James said very politely.

"How do you do young ladies? By any chance, did you bring my cheaters?"

"Your cheaters?" echoed Poppy.

"Yes, my cheaters, my spectacles....my eyeglasses."

Poppy focused with all her might on the cheetah's face. She seemed to be smiling. Poppy peered at the muscular cat's spots, her furry ears, her large paws that gripped the top of the boulder serving as her perch. She gazed into her golden eyes and down the dark tear marks that edged her broad flat nose. It was her eyes that had the greatest effect upon Poppy. She became more relaxed. Firinne's deep golden eyes shone with a mixture of kindness, curiosity and a glimmer of humor.

Ella broke the silence.

"She has them in her overalls. In the front pocket."

"You mean *these*?" Poppy held the antique glasses in front of her, high enough for Firinne to see.

"WHY YES!!!" Firinne exclaimed, jumping down from the ledge, motivating both girls to crouch behind the low bush blueberries. "I'm *very* excited!" She gracefully and noiselessly strolled by the bushes heading away from the girls, moving further down the trail. "I haven't seen them in *so* very long. They have been missing for quite some time. Somehow, eventually, they always seem to reappear, just when they are needed! Come and see.... I mean really *see*.... what they can do."

Poppy and Ella cautiously emerged from the blueberry bushes and followed the cheetah for quite a while. The trail sloped downward and the scattered sunbeams that poked through the canopy began to lessen as the day approached its end. With a few more twists and turns, the girls found themselves in a very dimly lit grove. Their senses suddenly were filled with the intoxicating smell of roses, the splashing of water against rock and the soft caress of a light breeze in their hair. Although Poppy and Ella imagined they were in a beautiful place, the twilight muffled their surroundings. As they walked further into the grove, they saw a magnificent waterfall, its water cascading off the cliff above, spilling into a small pool and then gliding over the rocks below, forming a stream that stretched out of sight. The edge of the pool was rimmed with four pillars of stone. Firinne walked to the first pillar and sat, winding her spotted tail around herself to shield her paws from the spray of the waterfall.

"Come closer to the pillar and tell me what you see," she said to Poppy and Ella.

They cautiously approached the first pillar and peered at it in the dim light.

"Tiny holes, in patterns," said Poppy.

"Like the ones we found on the papers… in the desk," added Ella.

"Now put the cheaters on," Firinne said.

Ella nudged Poppy, who looked confused. "She means the eyeglasses."

"*Ooooh*," Poppy said, removing the glasses from her pocket and looping the thin brass wire over her ears. Poppy's eyes widened and her tiny mouth hung open. She forgot all about the hole patterns she was supposed to be looking at. Her brain was too busy soaking in the spectacular scene that her eyes were seeing. A burst of sunshine brought the garden to life and warmed Poppy's cheeks. The falling, dancing water was sparkling in the brilliant sunlight. She was surrounded by hundreds of roses in shades of pink, purple, red, and yellow. Their brilliant color and delicious scent infiltrated Poppy's senses. Butterflies and bees hovered, too busy with the flowers to be bothered by the visitors.

"What do you see?" asked Ella excitedly.

Poppy handed the cheaters to Ella, who twirled in circles taking in the scenery.

"This is amazing!"

"The glasses change everything!" Poppy agreed.

"Although you are excited to see your surroundings differently, the cheaters can be problematic. I advise you to take them off until I can explain what they do," Firinne cautioned Ella.

Ella didn't want to take off the magical glasses, however one glance into Firinne's eyes made her realize she was telling the truth. Ella removed the cheaters.

"These cheaters, cheat. They show us what we do not normally see. Those who are in darkness are shown the light, and can see what they normally would have missed. However, the difficulty may lie in the fact that the cheaters show *too* much and can overwhelm the wearer. What one person sees through the lenses, may be very different than what another wearer might see. Not unlike the Chatterbox World, the magic of the cheaters is constantly changing. New images that are occurring in the present begin to mix with those from the past and then intertwine with images of what may come. The cheaters adapt; the goal is to illuminate the Chatterbox World for those who seek truth in their life."

"That's pretty heavy stuff!" Ella said, looking a little suspiciously at the glasses. "Here you take 'em back Pops."

The girls had been so engrossed with how their surroundings looked, they had forgotten that

Firinne had asked them to examine the pillars. Poppy took the cheaters from Ella, placed them on her face and peered at the patterns of tiny holes. In the place of each hole, was now a letter. She read what was written out loud:

"To view the world with a loving heart is a difficult task indeed"

She ran to the next pillar.

"To find the courage in challenging times may be just what you need"

Ella raced over to the third pillar.

"Pops, can I use the cheaters?"

Poppy handed them over.

"To think things through and use your mind especially in times of strife," Ella read aloud.

Ella grabbed Poppy's hand and pulled her to the last pillar. She opened her mouth to read the last line but Firinne beat her to it.

"To ride the waves of change and challenge are the keys to living your life," Firinne recited in her dark husky voice.

Poppy and Ella turned and looked at the cheetah expecting more, but she sat very still gazing right through them with a faraway look.

"Why are there holes in the stones instead of letters and why can we read what is written *only* with the glasses?"

"A very good question Poppy," the cheetah answered with a quick smile. "The Chatterbox Girl who came *before* you, saw things a little differently than you do."

"There's *another* Chatterbox Girl?!" both girls asked together.

"Why yes," Firinne said, curling the edges of her mouth up and wrinkling her nose. "Many have traveled through Chatterbox World before you and I suppose many will do so after. You are not alone. I've been told that the previous Chatterbox Girl needs the help of both of you in order to find her way back home."

This made Poppy's heart race and her cheeks bloomed a deep rose color just thinking about what Firinne had said.

"There's another chatterbox girl waiting for us out there somewhere and she needs our help!" Poppy gazed at Ella with her most serious face while Ella bobbed her head in agreement.

CHAPTER 13

YOU ARE WHAT YOU EAT

Ella and Poppy, exhausted from the day's wildly extraordinary events, had curled up under a tree very close to the cheetah, who provided them with warmth and a feeling of safety. They both slept very deeply, dreaming fragmented dreams filled with bespectacled cats and dancing daisies. When they awoke, Firinne was nowhere in sight and James now stood in her place, staring at them with his head cocked to one side looking deep in thought.

"You must be very parched and super hungry," James said to Ella, who had woken first.

"My stomach *is* rumbling," Ella agreed, wobbling still half asleep toward the water's edge. She cupped her hands together and drank deeply from the cool water.

"I could eat a horse!" Poppy shouted, stretching her arms and following Ella to the stream.

James closed his eyes and twisted his furry face in disgust. "That's *revolting* Poppy.... simply revolting."

Poppy and Ella started giggling, which turned into full blown laughter mixed with watery eyes.

"I'm only kidding! It's a thing people say!" Poppy sputtered while still laughing at the cat.

"Well please *don't* say it again!" James snapped at the girls. "I have some VERY close friends who are horses and...."

"Wait!" Ella interrupted James, putting a finger to her lips silencing the cat mid-sentence.

They could hear the wind chimes again. The tone was unmistakable. It was exactly the same noise they had heard the day before. The musical sound of the metal was coming closer and now it was mixed with the clanging and banging of something else and the grinding of wheels upon the rough path. Then suddenly it stopped. Ella and Poppy peered beyond the beautiful garden, deep into the forest.

"Somebody's out there," whispered Ella to Poppy.

"I'm scared!" Poppy whispered back, her eyes round with fear.

Both girls scanned the garden for James but the cat had disappeared while they were distracted.

"Maybe James went to check it out."

"Maybe," Ella said warily.

"Come on, let's follow the trail and look for more blueberries, I'm really starting to get hungry."

The two girls made their way out of the garden and down a steep slope that rimmed the edge of the mountain. They chose their steps carefully as the path dropped precariously off to one side.

"We're a long way up. I'd hate to fall off the cliff," Poppy said a little shakily, still thinking about the noise in the woods.

"Follow me and stay close. Hopefully the path will widen ahead."

"Ok El."

After a steep decline along the drop off, the path turned in toward the mountain through an opening in the rock. The rocky crevice led the two girls into another field, but this time there was not a daisy in sight. Poppy and Ella were both very pleasantly surprised to see rows and rows of vegetables planted in the bright sunshine in the middle of the field. They ran full speed with the warm sun beating down upon them, toward the delicious feast that awaited. Plopping herself down in the middle of the carrots, Poppy pulled the bushy tops from the soil and rubbed the carrots back and forth on her overalls, brushing the dirt from the orange skin. Ella had unearthed some juicy looking radishes and was also prying open some pea pods and popping the tiny green snacks into her mouth.

"Whooooa!" Poppy said pointing to an enormous red tomato.

"This is almost as good as Mamo's vegetable garden!" Ella remarked in between crunches, as she devoured a radish.

Mamo was well known in town for her amazing vegetable garden which she used in her daily cooking as well as shared with all her neighbors.

"We should rinse everything off in the stream," Ella said, loading both their pockets and filling their arms with what they had picked.

The girls cleaned the vegetables in the cool rushing stream water which skirted the edge of the field. They sat beside the water and munched on the delicious fresh vegetables. Poppy was enjoying the juicy mouth-watering red tomato but decided to mix things up by finishing the giant carrot she had started. She paused midbite and stared at Ella. Her mouth was still full and hanging open, but she couldn't quite manage to swallow.

"What are you staring at?" Ella asked, while still crunching on her favorite radishes.

"Your, your, your hair...." Poppy sputtered pointing at Ella's spiraled curls.

"What's wrong with my hair?!" Ella jumped to her feet trying to pull one of her spirals close to her eye.

"It's ppppink!" Poppy shouted, spilling vegetables all around her as she hopped to her feet.

"YOUR hair is turning orange!" Ella screeched, wide eyed and muffling a laugh.

"Your eyes aren't brown any more.... they're bright GREEN!" Poppy shrieked.

"And YOURS are turning bright red! *Ooooo* you look SCARY!"

"What is happening to us?!" Poppy jumped up and down with excitement mixed with a tinge of fear.

"I think it's the veggies! They're changing our hair and eyes to mimic their color!"

"This is SO COOL!!"

Poppy snatched a pea pod and ate all five peas that were hiding inside. Her eyes slowly changed from red to green. She ate two more bites from the tomato and her orange hair turned a bright red. The two girls ran back and forth between the vegetable garden and the stream, taking bites from the different vegetables they found, altering their appearance, screaming and jumping up and down with each dramatic change. James had emerged from the tall spindly grasses on the other side of the stream and sat shaking his furry head, snickering and rolling his eyes.

"Ooooo my stomach hurts," moaned Poppy.

"Well, what a surprise!" James said sarcastically.

"I'm definitely full," Ella nodded in agreement.

"Well, Mamo always says…. You are what you eat! She's definitely right when it comes to *this* garden!"

The two girls laid on their backs, by the edge of the stream on either side of James, soaking up the warm sun. They watched the dragon flies dance in the afternoon breeze. Ella thought she could hear the tinkling of wind chimes mixed in with the noises of the meadow, but then again, she wasn't really sure.

CHAPTER 14

THE LEGEND OF GRA

After a short rest, with their stomachs now full and having taken a long drink from the stream, the girls continued their journey with James in tow. They followed the path back into the woods as it wound down and around the mountain. James was usually at their side, but disappeared from time to time if he heard a noise in the forest, which he felt deemed investigation. The rays of sunlight poked through the canopy lighting their path and spectacular calls, unlike any they had heard before, came from the birds overhead. They approached a fork in the road.

One path fell sharply down to the left toward the edge of the mountain, while the other veered to the right continuing through the woods.

"Which way should we go?" Ella interrupted Poppy's thoughts.

"I was just thinking the same thing....and that Mamo must be worried about us." "How long have we been here?"

"I don't really know. I seem to have lost track of time.... like time seems different here."

The two girls decided to follow the path to the right, trudging on, mulling over these thoughts and some more.... like, *where are the boys? what are they doing? are they looking for us?*" The day wore on and nothing too eventful happened. The afternoon sun was replaced by a full moon which illuminated the forest. Both girls were happy to take another rest by the stream that seemed to snake its way along the path, disappear for a while and then return. They took another long drink and rested their backs on a comfortable bed of pine needles, looking up at the tree tops and the tiny bits of inky night sky.

"I've got this strange feeling that we're being watched," Poppy whispered to Ella.

"By James?"

"No, I saw him walk into the woods right before we stopped for a drink."

Poppy searched the ceiling of shadowy tree limbs and leafy green leaves but didn't see anything......but then a small movement caught her eye. Lying still, not moving, she whispered quietly to Ella to look up and to the right, to the largest tree in the area. Ella caught sight of a very large barn owl perched on a limb of the tree, his brown and grey feathers disguising him as part of the bark. It was his huge round blinking eyes and the movement of his feathers in the breeze that gave him away. His gaze was focused directly upon them. Ella held her breath.

"I see it," she said through her teeth as she slowly exhaled.

"It doesn't look dangerous."

"But it's definitely looking right at us."

Just as Poppy spoke her last word, the magnificent owl spread its wings and glided down to a branch much closer to the girls.

"I am Gra," the owl told them in a thick powerful tone.

"I'm Poppy and this is Ella," she told the bird moving only her finger to point to her friend.

"I'm very pleased to meet you. I hope your journey has gone well so far. I have heard very pleasant things about you."

Neither Poppy nor Ella could think of a thing to say, so they both remained quiet and waited for the owl to speak again.

"What do you think of Chatterbox World?" Gra asked, rotating his feathery head so far, the girls were frightened it would snap off.

"It's quite beautiful," answered Ella quietly.

"The vegetables make your hair and eyes turn colors," Poppy added with a small smile.

"Ahhhh yes, I do know what you mean." A flicker of amusement appeared on his face and then disappeared so quickly that Poppy was not sure she had actually seen it.

"We're looking for the *other* Chatterbox Girl......have you seen her?" Poppy asked hopefully.

"Why yes I have," the grand owl responded as he flew to a lower branch directly over the girls.

"How did she get here? Why does she need us to help her get home?" Ella asked, sitting up and craning her neck to get a better look at Gra.

"I'm quite sure she got here the same way you did. I think you will have to ask *her* why she needs your help to get home. Have you read her story?"

"Her story?" both girls said at once.

"Yes, everyone has a story. Yours is being written as we speak!"

"Where is it being written?" Poppy asked a little confused.

"Why of course in the book!"

"What book?"

"The book that holds all the stories of Chatterbox World!"

"Hmmmm, and where do we find this book?" Ella suddenly chimed in.

"Well, I believe you should ask the tinker," said Gra cocking his head to one side. "Have you seen him in your travels? He has a wooden cart with a covered top pulled by a sturdy horse named Cob. The cart is loaded with many useful things which make a terrible racket in the forest when the tinker is on the move.... pots and pans rattling and wind chimes clanging...."

"Yes, we've seen him!" Ella shouted jumping up in excitement. "Well at least we've *heard* him from a distance."

"We were afraid he was someone dangerous," Poppy told Gra.

"Oh no, he isn't dangerous. He is actually the original keeper of the chatterbox. No one really knows where he comes from and where he is going, but he seems to appear when he is most needed. He carries the book containing all the stories of Chatterbox World. He knows how much I love this world and its history, so when his travels take him by this part of the forest, he lets me read the new chapters that have been written in the book. I have a photographic memory and I memorize the stories. He relies on me to be the keeper of *all* the stories in case something should happen to the book. You can ask me about anything that has happened involving Chatterbox World and I will be able to tell you the story. I know them all by heart."

The girls were both very impressed by this talent and quickly seized the opportunity to learn about the other Chatterbox Girl.

"Please Gra, could you tell us the story of the other Chatterbox Girl?" asked Poppy.

"Oh, this is very exciting! I would love to! It's been quite a while since I was asked to narrate a tale from the tinker's book!"

Gra fluffed up his feathers and closed his eyes, clearing his throat and wiggling his tail feathers to get a little more comfortable on his perch. The girls scurried to the base of the next tree and sat with their backs against it for support, clasping their hands tightly together in excitement.

"Quite a long time ago," the great horned owl began, with his enormous eyes now fixed upon Ella and Poppy.

"Timothy was 13 years old when he became homeless. His father had died in the war and his mother, who had raised him alone and worked as a local bar maid, died of consumption on Timothy's 13th birthday."

Ella, looking a little confused, poked Poppy and both girls shrugged.

"Mr. Gra," Poppy interrupted. We want to know about the Chatterbox Girl, not a boy named Timothy."

"To know about the life of the Chatterbox Girl, you must also learn about Timothy, as their lives are very intertwined"

The girls nodded and decided to keep quiet. Gra cleared his voice once again and continued his story:

"It's hard to say what a boy of 13 who found himself alone in the world would think of all this. He had been extremely close to his mother and had for the past year, worked at the local grist mill doing manual labor to help pay for the tiny room they rented and the groceries that kept them alive. To his credit he was a very hard worker, always prompt and eager to work extra hours when needed. This and his easy-going quiet manner put him in good graces with the owner of the mill, who after his mother died, offered Tim a small room in the back of his barn usually used for hay storage. This tiny room and the job he had at the mill, were enough to keep his spirit alive and the

125

courage to keep going in life. He had a natural love for animals and without even being asked, would often tend to the sheep and the few cows and chickens that shared the barn with him.

The owner of the gristmill, a rugged Irishman named John, lived alone with his daughter Mary, who was 6 years younger than Tim. His wife had died during childbirth and John had struggled greatly to keep his mill going while still taking care of little Mary. Mary had been born blind and although this made his love and desire to protect his little girl even stronger, raising her and giving her the best life he could, was going to be quite a challenge for her father. He hired a local woman named Maggie to take care of her while he was at the mill. As she got older, he found it more difficult to be apart from his daughter during the long hours he spent at work. Mary was a beautiful little girl and it was often said that it was her smile that kept her father's heart beating.

When she was a toddler, John would take her to the office at the grist mill, and let her play on the floor with her toys, while he worked the grinding stone and kept a close eye on the work at hand. John and the workers at the mill, Aiden and Sean, would take turns checking on her. She was well loved by the men and lunchtime was full of laughter, as she bounced on their knees and shared bites from their lunches and giggled at the crazy songs they made up and sang to her. They were constantly trying to outdo one another to get her to laugh the hardest. John would have to break up the banter by bellowing 'back to work!' at the top of his lungs. It would take him quite some time to settle Mary and get her to lie in her little wooden bed tucked in the corner of the office. She wanted to follow her father into the mill to listen to the mesmerizing spinning of the mechanisms and wheels. But a tiny bottle of milk and a story would usually close her unseeing eyes for a much-needed rest.

It would have been easier for John, had he left Mary at the house each day with Maggie, but he couldn't bear to be away from her so much and wanted her to be a part of his days.

When Timothy came to work at the mill, Mary was 7 years old. She spent most of her time in the office, listening to the little Victrola her father had purchased for her birthday, while dancing and singing to her dolls. Timothy soon became Mary's favorite as they were closer in age. She would follow him around the barn while he took care of the animals, and he whittled her a little wooden chicken out of a broken piece of barn board. She carried her little chicken wherever she went and there were many tears and no sleep if Chicken was mislaid. Timothy had a knack for storytelling and many a night she would fall asleep to his tales; of animals of the forest both terrifying and wonderful and the adventures they had when grownups were not around. By his 14th birthday,

Timothy was living in the spare room of the house and had become more of a son to John, than just a laborer at the mill. Tim was so grateful to have a place to live where he felt loved, and he admired John more than any other person he had ever met. On the other hand, John had grown attached to the young boy, and grew to love his company, and of course was very glad Mary had someone nearer her age to be with. Timothy liked bringing home 'little prizes' to Mary from the travelling tinker that came to town once every few weeks."

Gra closed his moon shaped eyes and paused to preen himself. He rotated his large feathery head almost 180 degrees and peered up at the brilliantly bright full moon. After what seemed like a very long time to Poppy and Ella, he slowly rotated his fluffy dome to gaze once again upon the two girls.

Poppy and Ella remained silent, afraid to interrupt his tale, but Ella could take the lapse no more.

"Is there more Gra?" she nervously inquired.

"Why yes, there is Ella," he answered tilting his head in an affectionate way.

Poppy smiled hopefully and leaned forward to listen.

Gra began again:

"The tinker was an unusual little man with dark brown eyes and grey scraggly hair. His back was bent with age and he wore a crooked smile on his face. His tinker's cart was filled with all kinds of goods, both ordinary and unusual. Everything from useful housewares to unusual finds from the tinker's travels were to be found on his horse drawn wooden cart. Pots and pans, large spoons, knives, hatchets and buckets all hung from the wooden pegs on his cart and made a terrible racket that alerted the townspeople that he was back in town. He also had mystical bottles with colorful labels, all claiming to be a cure for anything from the common cold to toothaches. The tinker kept a small dome topped trunk under the base of his cart. It was in this trunk that he secured his 'special' items.

He was very choosy who he shared these hidden treasures with. It was rumored that the tinker had magical powers and was hundreds of years old. He would disappear from town as quickly as he would reappear weeks later. No one ever saw him actually come or go. Many were too frightened to buy his wares because of their fear of the unknown, but there were others who were drawn to his cart out of curiosity and were very pleased indeed, since he tended to have just what was needed. Timothy was one of the few customers that the tinker actually spoke more than a few words to. He often asked the young man about his life and the work he did at the grist mill. Each time the tinker would come to town, Tim would ask him if he had anything that Mary might like. His recent acquisition from the tinker was a small round metal spinning top. Timothy was very excited to give it to Mary and thanked the tinker profusely, shaking his tiny hand up and down, promising to tell him what Mary thought of the top the next time he visited. Timothy muddled through his thoughts as he left the tinker that bright shining day. He couldn't help thinking about the argument between the newly married Mrs. Truffles and the sweet, young Mrs. Quackenberry, he had overheard at the butcher shop. Mrs. Truffles thought the tinker looked like her Uncle Herbert, who was a tall gangly man with droopy eyes. While Mrs. Quackenberry insisted he was quite pudgy and round with a balding head. Neither woman would give in nor agree. And then the argument ended abruptly when Mrs. Temsley, who had been eavesdropping from the back of the shop, piped in that she thought he was quite young and handsome. All three women had paused with a look of concern and confusion on their face and then quickly changed the subject to who should win this year's pie contest.

Mary squealed with delight and gave Tim the strongest bear hug she could muster when he presented her with the little top. Her father told Tim that he was spoiling the girl and gave him a concerned look, but it was only meant to cover the small smile that played upon his lips. The next day was rainy and cool, so Mary spent the afternoon sitting at her father's desk in the mill office, playing with the little metal top that Timothy had given her. She loved the feel of the smooth tin slipping quickly through her hands and the whirring sound it made as she pumped the little handle at the top. It kept her busy while the men worked in the mill. After playing with her new top for a little while, Mary became bored and decided to go outside. She carried her chicken carefully down the stairs and tilted her head in the morning sun, listening for the song of the birds nearby. She could smell the fragrant aroma of the lilac bushes on the river bank as they whispered and swayed in the light breeze.

Carefully edging her way toward the intoxicating scent, she held her little hands out in front of her, trying to feel her way to the soft petals and smooth texture of the lilacs.

Meanwhile, the men were doing the backbreaking job of carrying the sacks of flour from the ground floor and then loading them onto the trucks. Tim, Sean and Aiden were hard at work on the bottom floor, while John worked the grain into the hopper from above. It was some time before any of them were able to check on Mary and suddenly Tim heard a heart stopping scream, that seemed to come from the river. His whole body became cold with fear. It was as if the freezing mill water was coursing through his veins. Dropping his flour sack and tearing to the water's edge, he frantically searched the river but could not see anything amiss. The wheel was turning freely. Just then another muffled scream came from the base of the wheel, where it connected through to the mill. Timothy dove into the icy water and lurched forward with all his might, fighting the churning waves. Sean repeatedly bellowed 'stop the wheel!' while Aiden flung his body toward the mill door, all the while begging at the top of his lungs for John to break the wheel. Mary desperately thrashed about in the water. Her dress was caught on the base of the wheel and she was being pulled under the frigid depths with every turn. Tim managed to grab the hem of Mary's dress and hold her close just as the wheel stopped turning. He pulled the little girl across the water to the river's edge, using every bit of strength he had. She was shaking and coughing, spitting up little gulps of water and crying all at the same time. Aiden and Sean were already by Mary's side wrapping her in the blanket from the work truck. John flew down the stairs insane with raging fear that he had lost his precious little girl, but Timothy had saved her life."

The majestic owl began to sway on the branch that held his formidable frame. Gra closed his eyes and he became both narrator and the host of voices from the past. Both the events and words spoken spilled eerily from his curved beak:

"I'm so sorry Tim,' was the first thing she stuttered from her little blue lips.

'Don't talk,' whispered Tim, 'we'll take you down to the house and Maggie will get you warm by the fire.'

It was then that Mary started to sob uncontrollably. She was so upset. Nothing they said seemed to calm her down. She buried her face in Tim's soft work shirt and cried so hard her whole body was shaking with the strain.

'Calm down Mary,' Tim quietly consoled her as he rocked his body back and forth to comfort not only Mary, but himself as well.

'It's so awful Tim,' Mary choked the words out through her tears.

'You're going to be ok,' he said with a small smile.

'I lost Chicken!' she shrieked full of heartbreak and loss.

'What? O Mary,' he said relieved. 'I can make you another chicken.'

"Nooooooo I want myyyy chicken she wailed!'

Mary cried the whole way back to the house and she could not be consoled about her lost chicken. She didn't even seem to mind that she had almost drowned in the river. She fell asleep wrapped in Maggie's arms, as the woman rocked the little girl to sleep by the fire. The last thing she said before she dropped off to sleep was, 'my chicken can't swim."

Gra paused. Only the chirping crickets could be heard. He was breathing more deeply now, his multi-layered chest pumping up and down.

"It's kinda weird hearing those voices come out of an owl," whispered Poppy.

"Shhhhh!" Ella put her finger to her lips. "He might hear you and we won't know how it ends!"

But the owl, in his trancelike state, continued:

"'Tim, I need to talk with you.' John stared into the boy's eyes intently, over the breakfast table the next morning. Mary's father had not slept a minute the night before and his eyes were rimmed with dark circles, making his stare seem even more intense than usual. 'I'm closing the mill for a few weeks. We are ahead of schedule and I have another project that needs to be done.'

Tim simply nodded and listened to what John had to say. He was exhausted as well from the stress of the day before. After poking his head into Mary's room and reassuring himself that she was safely asleep in her bed, he slumped into a chair at the kitchen table listlessly watching Maggie cook eggs and slice her homemade bread.

'There's an old tunnel that runs along the river. It was built by my grandfather and father almost 100 years ago and used as a mill chase. It was closed off and the river water was rerouted before I was born. A

grain storage cabin was then added to the end of the tunnel. I haven't set eyes on it since I was a kid. I'd like to go look for it and see what condition it's in. If it's not too far gone, I'd like to restore it and make it into a playhouse for Mary. It's made of stone so there might be a chance it's still salvageable. After breakfast, meet Aiden and Sean at the mill and tell them about my plans. Gather some tools together and meet me by the river's edge at the end of the back field. You'll all be paid your usual wage.'

Tim was feeling quite unwell and completely lacking in energy. He wondered how he would be able to work at all that day, and could only manage to say 'Yes sir.' He swallowed the piece of toast in his mouth with much difficulty and pushing his chair back noisily, staggered back to his room. He had no interest in this new project and really couldn't think of anything but the scene in his head: Mary clutching to the base of the waterwheel and the icy water that coursed through his veins and drenched his clothes as he desperately, with all his strength and might, had willed himself to save her. 'How could that ever have happened?' he whispered to himself. Up to that moment he had not cried, but tears started rolling down his cheeks as he walked to the tool shed. He spent more than a few minutes sobbing into the thick wool coat of one of the sheep in the barn. Looking a little confused, the sheep trotted away. Tim collected himself as best as he could and then carried out what John had asked him to do.

There was much work to be done to restore the grain house. After several hours of clearing years of overgrowth from the little building, the men evaluated what needed to be done.

'I had forgotten it had eight sides,' John mumbled aloud.

Aiden and Sean continued to clear brush and briars away and made a wide walking path around the tiny house. John walked its perimeter, knocking his knuckles against the side of the old bulkhead out back, sliding his large calloused fingers over the smooth fieldstone surface, surrounding the beautifully crafted arched wooden door and its hand forged handle. Tim limberly climbed the wooden ladder he had propped against the side of the structure. After careful evaluation, he decided what needed to be done. The metal roof required patching and was in desperate need of a coat of paint. After a quick round trip back to the field, Timothy patched a few thin rusty spots and slathered the red paint left over from the barn onto the old tin, brightening up and sealing the roof. He was careful of the glass in the large oversized skylight that had been installed in the roof many years ago to let the sun shine into the house, keeping the grain dry and mildew free. Tim plopped down on the damp prickly ground and shaded his eyes, cocking his head to one side and taking in the tiny structure.

'It's a sweet little house,' he commented to John.

'Let's look inside,' John answered, as he pushed the heavy door inward.

Tim jumped up and quickly followed, eager to see what was inside the long-forgotten house. In the dim, grimy light that filled the single room, Tim could see the floor was littered with old grain sacks. A large wooden cupboard, originally used to store homemade jelly and canned goods, stood against the rounded rocks. Next to it, was a wooden door with black hinges and a brass doorknob. Tim assumed this was the entrance to the tunnel. But the cupboard was dwarfed by the enormous hand carved desk that stood against the opposing wall. Timothy stared, admiring the massiveness of the desk and the quirky cat faced drawer handles that decorated the front.

'If I remember correctly,' John said to Tim, 'the locking code to this door is my father's birthday: 3-6-

58.' He pushed the corresponding brass buttons in, unlocking the door.

The next few weeks were spent cleaning and repairing the little house and adding supports to the attached tunnel. John had not been forthcoming as to his exact plans for the former grain house and tunnel, but at the end of the second week he invited Sean, Aiden and Tim to the farmhouse kitchen. Over a pot roast dinner prepared by Maggie, he revealed his ideas to the men.

'I've been foolish letting Mary stay alone in the office while we work. We almost lost her and this made me realize she is getting too old and it's getting too dangerous to leave her alone. I want to use this little cabin as a playhouse for her while we are working. It's somewhere she can be in the daytime that is her own. Because of the tunnel she will not have to go outside to come see us and she will be safe. Maggie wants to give her sewing lessons. We can bring my *mother's old sewing machine down to the playhouse so she has something to work with. Maggie tells me that although being blind, she can learn to sew. She could work as a seamstress when she gets older and be able to make some money on her own.'*

There was silence at the table for a few minutes as the men took all this in. They all felt responsible for the little girl and loved her very dearly. Breaking the silence suddenly, Tim said rather enthusiastically;

'I think it's a great plan! It will take a little while to make it all work, but Mary might like having her own little house. She can be very stubborn and I don't know if she will mind not being at the mill with us though,' he added.

'Well let's give it a try,' agreed Aidan, as he stood up and made his way toward the old treadle sewing machine that was tucked in the corner of the kitchen."

"It was a remarkable success," Gra continued, snapping out of his trance for a moment and cocking his head at the girls. It was only for a moment, however, as he once again closed his knowing eyes and continued:

"Mary loved her little playhouse and the independence it gave her. She became an avid seamstress and at a very young age began to make her own money doing repairs and alterations for the locals, earning a modest income. But the most important gift she received in her young life was from Tim. He acquired the precious, small domed topped trunk from the tinker. The day was cold, dark and rainy. He was bundled up keeping an even pace to his step, as he walked back from town on an errand to buy groceries for Maggie, when the tinker appeared seemingly out of nowhere.

'This is a sad day for a walk,' the tinker spoke in a musical tone.

'Groceries are needed regardless of the weather,' was Tim's response.

'How is your Mary?' the tinker queried Tim with narrowing eyes.

'She is well, my Tinker. She is happy.'

'Does she feel at home in her octagonal cabin? Does she treasure the stories you have pinned for her?'

'How might you know about my pinned alphabet and my stories?'

'I have a special sense for great acts of love; unusual and imaginative things that make another's life worth living. These events are very rare in this difficult world in which you live. They shine brightly amidst an often dark and cold existence, not unlike the stars which shine in an inky black sky.' The tinker gazed into Tim's face. It was spattered with rain but the tinker could see into the light of his eyes. He noticed what others missed.

'I have something for Mary,' he said quietly to Tim, bending down and dragging the tiny domed trunk with a locking key, that rested on the bottom *frame of his cart. 'This is for her cabin. It contains only one treasure; the most extraordinary of all my treasures. It is one of the greatest gifts you can give to another; a future filled with love and hope. Although you will not always be together, it will intertwine your lives and you will find each other again.'*

'I'm not sure what you mean kind Tinker, but I will deliver your gift to Mary with pleasure and I am sure she will treasure it as she has done with all your past gifts.'

'Those were not my gifts to give, Tim. I have traveled the world for more years than you'd want to count, searching for the next home for my domed trunk and its contents. The very first time I met you, and you spoke of your friend Mary, I knew my task was done.'

Placing the tiny trunk in a satchel bag, Tinker patted Tim on the back and wished him well. After

20 paces or so, Tim turned back to wave goodbye to the tinker, but he was now quite alone."

The owl no longer spoke. His eyes remained closed so the girls were not sure if they should say anything. This time Poppy broke the silence.

"Everything is starting to make sense now. So *that's* where the little trunk and the chatterbox came from!"

"Yes! The chatterbox and the tinker are the only gateways *into* this world. There is only one way out."

"One way out?" Poppy echoed Gra.

"Yes," said Gra shifting his eyes to hers. "This world is designed for those who enter, to seek out that which is most important to them. When the Chatterbox Girl finds the true answer to her dilemma, she will find her way out. It seems as if you have a valuable and intelligent ally with you. You choose your friends well, Chatterbox Girl. That, in itself is a valuable life lesson to many; for who you choose to spend your days with, greatly effects the twists and turns in your life."

"I think he just complimented me," Ella whispered, nudging Poppy with her elbow.

"I think so too," giggled Poppy. "My head has too many words crammed into it."

"I think I know what you mean," Ella said still gazing at the owl.

Gra snickered and puffed out his feathers.

The girls were exhausted from the day's events. They laid down on a soft bed of moss under Gra's tree and fell asleep to the song of the katydids. They both dreamed magical nonsensical dreams filled with all the characters from Gra's story. In the earliest morning hours, Poppy awoke for only a moment and thought; *"I want to help Mary find her way back home."*

Poppy and Ella awoke to a songbird singing its very best tune in the nearby bushes. Mr. Cat; that is James, was standing nearby in a patch of sunlight, inspecting the fur on his tail and humming softly to himself.

"We met Gra last night!" Poppy told the unsuspecting cat, who seemed to be too involved with his own thoughts to notice the girls had awoken.

"You did, did you?" he said with a smirk. "I bet the old bird had your ears ringing with his endless stories."

"Well he *did* tell us the story of the other Chatterbox Girl. Her name is Mary! The cabin in the woods, the tunnel and the grist mill are all part of her story!!! And all those pin holes in the papers and on the stones were made for her!"

"She can't see like we do," Ella added.

"Ahhhh yes. It's easy to forget that she cannot see. She gets around quite well in this world."

"You know her? You've seen her?" the girls asked James.

"Yes, of course I know her. I know everyone in Chatterbox World!" James shook his head and rolled his eyes as usual.

"Can you take us to her?" Poppy pleaded jumping with excitement.

"Where is Gra? I don't see him anywhere in the trees," Ella said, scanning the leaves and branches above, while shading her eyes from the ever-increasing sunlight.

"He's not a morning person. Sleeps all day and is on forest watch from dusk 'til dawn."

"Oh, I wish I could say goodbye and thank him for his company and wonderful story."

"I'll let him know next time I'm in this neck of the woods," James said with a quick smile.

With that comment, James turned tail and started ambling down the path, away from the girls. Rushing to scoop a mouthful of water from the stream, they scurried after James' swishing tail, just as it rounded a turn and disappeared out of sight.

CHAPTER 15

BACK AT THE GRIST MILL

F inn, Charlie and Mike were having the time of their lives working in the river, removing the large rocks, tree limbs and dead logs that had fallen in or been dragged there by the current. All this debris had slowed the water flow and piled up against the mill's water wheel. The day was warm and sunny so they didn't mind being soaked in the cool river water. Even though Charlie's arm was no longer in a cast it was stiff and skinny. He gave it a real workout by dragging many water-soaked logs to the river's edge with Mike's help.

"We've made a lot of progress for one day," Finn shouted to Mike and Charlie. "It's getting close to dinner time. We should meet up with Poppy and Ella and see how they're doing."

They packed their bags, whistled and called for Toby. After a few minutes the dog came bounding out of the woods where he had been following the trail of who knows what. They headed back into the mill and made their way through the tunnel with the help of their flashlights, since the fuel in the wall lamps had burned out. Running up the set of stairs into the cabin, Finn was very surprised to find that the room was empty.

"Where do you think they are?" Charlie asked, a little out of breath, the last one into the room.

"They must be outside." Finn left the cabin and started calling their names.

"Look, they've definitely been here! The trunk is open!" Mike pointed to the little domed box.

"I can't find them anywhere," said Finn, panting as he ran back into the cabin. I called and called and there was no answer."

"What's *that* thing?" Charlie pointed to the chatterbox. It sat on the floor, resting on its side, next to the little domed trunk.

Finn bent over and picked up the chatterbox. It immediately started to glow. Toby began barking and jumping up to see what was in Finn's hand.

"Whoa what's going on?!" said Mike taking a step backwards.

"That's cool!" Charlie said, walking toward the glowing chatterbox in order to take a closer look.

Finn gently placed the chatterbox on the top of the desk and all three boys gathered around to take a closer look.

"Finn, is that one of those cootie catchers?"

"It sure looks like one."

"It's pretty fancy......it's glowing!"

"It's giving *me* the cooties," said Mike with a shiver.

"Everything gives you the cooties," Charlie said smirking at his friend.

"I've got a strange feeling that something's not right," Finn said in a worried tone, looking at Mike and Charlie. "Let's go back to the tents and see if the girls are there."

The only problem with their plan was that Toby wouldn't leave the cabin. He continued to bark at the chatterbox. Finn and Mike had to drag him out of the little house.

"What's wrong with you Toby?!" Finn asked the over excited pup. "We have to find Poppy and Ella!" Toby continued to bark, scratching at the door and whining. "Let's start walking back to the field and see if he follows."

They took off through the woods, and eventually Toby caught up with them, still barking and running in circles. When they reached their camp site and saw that the girls were not there, they really started to worry.

"We need to go back to the farmhouse and check for them there," Finn suggested.

"What are we gonna do if we can't find them?! What will we say to Mamo?!" Charlie asked feeling a little frantic.

"We'll just have to ask Mamo if we can have a picnic dinner out by the tents." Finn shrugged his shoulders.

"She's gonna get suspicious," said Mike shaking his head.

"Well we'll just have to be convincing." Finn looked very worried. "What's our other option? I'm not telling her we lost the girls. She doesn't even know we've been out in the woods."

The boys talked it over a little more and decided they had no choice but to check for the girls at the farmhouse and if they weren't there, try to get a picnic dinner and return as quickly as possible. They had to find Poppy and Ella. Finn's stomach was in knots just thinking about what he would say to Mamo. He had never lied to her before and he felt awful about doing it now. He knew if he told her the girls were missing, then everything they had been doing with the cabin and the mill would be found out. He approached the back-kitchen door, signaling Mike and Charlie to keep quiet. Peering in through the screen, he was relieved to see that Mamo was not in the kitchen and that dinner was not ready. He waved for Charlie and Mike to follow him into the house. Just as the door swung shut behind Charlie, they heard Seamus' voice coming from his office. He was on the telephone with a client, so they had time to sneak upstairs, look for the girls and change into dry clothes.

"Hey boys!" Seamus shouted up the stairs.

"O Hey Seamus!" Finn ran to the top of the stairway to talk with his father.

"Mamo went into town to have dinner with Ernie and Mr. Timpiste. She left us a tray of sandwiches and her home-made French fries in the kitchen. Help yourselves to anything you want. I'm on the phone with a client but I'll be done soon."

Finn felt the weight of the world lift off his shoulders. He could not believe how lucky they were that Mamo was out for the night. It was literally the best thing that could have happened.

"Hey Seamus......do you think we could pack up the sandwiches and fries and eat out at the tents with the girls tonight?"

"Ok by me," Seamus said with a smile. "Better get back soon before the girls get spooked. It's getting dark out."

When Finn returned to his bedroom, Charlie and Mike were jumping up and down clapping their hands and throwing themselves on the bed, without making a sound. They emptied their backpacks and repacked them with sweatshirts, including two from Poppy's room, flashlights, extra batteries, Finn's jackknife and compass. They crept down the stairs, filled the top of their packs with sandwiches and French fries, and snuck out the kitchen door. They ran across the field and back toward the tents, hooting and howling and all talking at once, about how lucky they were to escape without talking to Mamo.

"Where's Toby?" Mike asked, still panting from the run across the field.

"I don't think he followed us back to the house. The last time I remember seeing him was when we crossed the bridge," answered Charlie.

"Listen!" Finn cupped his ears, leaning forward. The boys walked toward the woods and stood still, straining their ears.

"It's Toby! I can hear him barking! It sounds like its coming from the cabin!" Mike shouted.

They dug out their flashlights and ran toward the woods. It was now almost completely dark outside, but thankfully the moonshine and their flashlights and the sound of Toby's barking lead them straight back to the little house. Toby became more frantic as he heard the boys approach.

"Okay, okay Toby!" Finn pushed open the door to the cabin and the pup burst into the room. He sat on the floor in front of the oversized desk and began to whine.

"He's looking at that cootie-catcher," said Mike.

"We don't have time for this," Charlie whined. "We have to find Poppy and Ella!"

"Wait.... what if this thing has to do with their disappearance." Finn picked up the chatterbox. It began to glow and brilliant colors oozed out of its triangular depths. Charlie and Mike both reached out to feel the smooth sides and peer into the faces of Mr. Cat and the cheetah wearing glasses. With a huge burst of light, the chatterbox fell to the floor, landing inches from Toby's feet. The poor pup was now alone in the octagonal cabin.

CHAPTER 16

MARY MARY LONELY MARY HOW DOES YOUR GARDEN GROW?

More than four decades before, while playing with the chatterbox that Timothy had given to her, Mary had entered Chatterbox World in the same way as Poppy and Ella. She was filled with both fear and wonder when she realized she was no longer in her playhouse, but in a different place altogether. Although she could not see with her eyes the delights that this world had to offer, her other senses of smell and touch and hearing were so developed, that she experienced the world in a way that no other traveler in this land had done before. The whispers of the wind among the daisies as they brushed lightly against her skin, the whirring of the dragonfly wings mixed with the light scent of earth and wildflowers, and the warm sun caressing her cheeks, eased her fear of not knowing where she was, or what had happened to the chatterbox she was playing with. She gently reached out toward the sound of soft purring to stroke James' big fluffy cheeks. He tilted his head and pushed against her small fingers, loving the caress of his favorite human.

"Where are we James?" she whispered to the cat.

This was one of James' favorite things about Mary; she was quiet and gentle, even her laughter was musical, unlike the loud chortling of most humans. He loved being near her, watching her sew in her little octagonal cabin. She never questioned where he came from or why he was there. She asked nothing of him, and that is *precisely* why he wanted to give the experience of Chatterbox World to her. It was his plan to do what he could, to help Mary find her way in the complex and foreboding world of humans.

"It's called Chatterbox World Mary," he answered moving closer to her side, slipping under her arm to comfort her. "It's not important *where* we are but *what* we experience here."

"I hear something approaching," she said with a slight tremor in her voice.

"It's only my friend Firinne. She is gentle and kind and has a gift for you."

The sleek and powerful cheetah parted the daisy stems as she approached Mary and James. She quietly laid down next to Mary and tilted her bespectacled face toward James, so that her eyeglasses slipped to the end of her broad nose. James snatched the cheaters with his mouth, careful not to scratch the lenses with his teeth and placed them on Mary's lap.

"These are cheaters; just like the ones you have helped your father put on his face many times at the mill. Put them on Mary"

Mary did as James asked. Suddenly her mind felt like it was exploding. The muscles in her body quivered. The feelings that swarmed over her brought goosebumps to her skin. She felt out of breath as her heart beat wildly. She could see. She could see the flowers, the sky, the dragonflies, colors that she had never even imagined existed. Tears streamed down her beautiful face as she looked into James' eyes and stroked his orange stripes. She couldn't speak. There were no words to fully describe the enormity of what she felt. Firinne and James remained quiet and gave Mary time to adjust to the world she had never actually seen before with her own eyes. Mary stood and took in her surroundings, soaking in all that was around her. The light and colors and movements were so brilliant, they began to overwhelm her and Mary's head began to ache.

"It's amazing. It's beautiful," she whispered. "I don't know if I like it."

James glanced at Firinne with a look of surprise.

"That's not what I expected you to say," he said to Mary.

"It's not the world I'm used to. It's almost too much to take in. Everything is so bright…. I don't know what…."

"You may keep them on or take them off, whatever you like Mary," said Firinne. "These glasses do not work in the world of humans, but in Chatterbox World they are very powerful. There are many wonderful things to see in both our worlds, and just as many things that are not worth seeing, especially in the human world. It is the beautiful things that Chatterbox World has to offer that I wish you to see and keep in your memory. A mind filled with positive images and memories can be helpful in troubled times. You will understand what I mean someday, when you need to draw upon your time in Chatterbox World."

"Let's go for a walk; get out of the sun for a while," James suggested.

Mary, Firinne and James entered the path into the forest of giant elms, oaks and cedar trees. Although Mary soaked in the images of the towering giants and the streams of sunlight poking through, she spoke to James and Firinne, only of the smell of the earth and trees and the cool breeze that slipped through her hair. She wasn't used to actually *seeing* what was around her, so she didn't really have the vocabulary to describe it. She remained very quiet in the grotto of roses, staring intensely at the colorful flowers and breathing in their fragrance. She saw the letters on the stone pillars as they formed the words; but it confused her. She took the glasses off and felt the tiny holes imbedded into the rock. The aching in her head started to subside right away. Firinne led her from one pillar to the next.

"Did Timothy write this for me?" she asked, after she recited the last verse aloud.

"No, it's something that was written many years ago in Chatterbox World. Some say the tinker wrote the verses, but no one is totally sure this is true. The words have always been written with letters of the alphabet, but they seem to have changed in form to your Timothy's pin holes."

Mary smiled. Timothy had devised an alphabet just for her, and had used it to teach her how to read. He used a large sewing pin that he borrowed from Maggie, to make holes in the pages of a small notebook he had acquired from the tinker. He didn't have access to the books used to teach the blind, so he made up a pattern for each letter and taught Mary the symbols for the 26 letters of the alphabet. The first 26 pages of the notebook held the alphabet while the next 10 were numbers. After she learned the letters, he taught her how to put them together and had her sound out the words. She was very quick to learn because she loved spending time with Tim and she was so eager to do something new. Tim wrote her one story per week. Mary would read the story out loud to Tim after dinner on Friday nights. Her father and Maggie would listen and marveled at the fact that Tim had taught her to read. Even though she later learned to read in braille, Mary never forgot how to read Tim's stories and kept the cherished book and papers.

"I don't understand the letters I see with the glasses," Mary told James and Firinne. "I much prefer Tim's writing."

With that comment, she slipped the cheaters into her cotton dress pocket and placed her hand on the smooth fur of Firinne's head. The brilliant colors of the grotto were now gone, but Mary listened to the sound of the falling water and rubbed her cheek against the cheetah's fur, feeling content again. Her head no longer hurt. Firinne led Mary along the path and eventually to the vegetable garden, where she ate and then drank from the stream and rested. She heard the clatter of wind chimes and the approaching cart of the tinker. He spoke with her quietly and told her he knew of a little log house where she could rest for the night. She was nervous at first, but with encouragement from James and Firinne and the promise that they would follow closely behind, she agreed to travel in the tinker's cart. When they reached the little house made of logs on the edge of the woods, Mary was feeling a bit lonely and scared; being away from her octagonal playhouse and Tim, her father and Maggie made her feel very unsettled. They were all that she had in the world and all that she knew.

James encouraged her to wear the cheaters until she became familiar with her surroundings. She wore them sparingly however, and mostly for a little while after dusk since she could not seem to get used to the brilliance of the sun, and the way they made her head ache. Night passed into day, and more days turned into what seemed like weeks. The tinker stayed close and Firinne and James never left Mary's side. She became so familiar with her surroundings that she stopped using the cheaters altogether; in fact, she had forgotten where they were. The tinker, who seemed to have endless supplies in his cart, made sure she had everything she needed and even shared his little muslin bags of magical seeds with Mary; teaching her how to make a garden where she grew delicious vegetables of all kinds. She took great pride in her garden and was amazed that she could create something so wonderful. She lost track of time and felt very happy during the daylight hours, but when she laid in bed at night she felt a pang of loneliness for Timothy, her father and Maggie. She even missed her octagonal cabin and her sewing machine. What bothered her most of all, what made her stomach churn and her throat so tight that she could barely swallow, was what she overheard one night in her bedroom back at home before she came to Chatterbox World. Shortly before she had arrived in Chatterbox World, Timothy and her father, John, were speaking in hushed tones in the kitchen outside her bedroom. What Timothy said that night to her father filled her with a dread she had never felt before. Timothy had told John, that he was thinking of joining the military to learn to fly. It was these words that made her feel lonelier than she had ever felt before. She didn't have friends her own age. She didn't go to school like the other kids in town. Her life was filled with the daily work at the mill and with her sewing, but it was Timothy who brought companionship, laughter, imagination and fun into her world. She was terrified he would go; but she was even more petrified that he would never return. This night, the fear of losing her best friend was too much for Mary. She lay in her little bed, clutching her knees, pulling them toward her chin, shaking and crying herself to sleep. It broke James' heart to see her pain and although he and Firinne and Tinker could not change what would happen in the world of humans, there was something they could give to Mary that would ease her pain and give her the strength and desire to live on. They could give her hope; hope for a life that would have its challenges, but one in which she knew she would be loved and needed and definitely not alone.

CHAPTER 17

NOPE FROG

T he red dirt path left the edge of the mountain and wound its way deep into the forest; so deep that it was darker and cooler than Poppy and Ella would have liked.

"I'm getting goose bumps I'm so cold," Poppy said, her teeth chattering.

"There's no sun in here and it smells kind of musty." Ella scrunched up her nose, rubbing her arms to warm herself. "The trees are changing too. Something isn't right…. I can feel it in me bones!"

The trees were different. They were thinner and weaker and bent over the pathway. The air was moist and chilly and darkness closed in around them with each step. The creatures of the night were starting to stir and the noises made the girls uncomfortable.

"Where's James?! That cat is always wandering off!" Ella complained, smacking at something on her back.

"There's bugs in here! You've got fireflies circling all around you!" Poppy made a face at Ella.

"Well you do too!" Ella shouted, waving her arms trying to smack away the pesky bugs.

The nasty little flying demons were definitely not fireflies, because they were attacking the girls and biting them, taunting each time they took a nip out of the girls' skin. They had long thin black bodies and red heads, with black piercing eyes. Their underbellies shone with a luminescent yellow glow making them easy for the girls to see in the lingering light. The more Poppy and Ella swung their arms the faster the bugs circled the girls, all the while piercing the night air with their shrill cackling.

"They're laughing at us! These flies are actually laughing at us!" Ella screamed and ran down the pathway trying to get away from the annoying insects.

Poppy raced after Ella and smacked an oversized, jeering, red faced bug sitting on Ella's back, squishing it against her. The result was a luminous yellow glowing stain on Ella's Dr Pepper t-shirt and Poppy's right hand.

"Ow!" shouted Ella. "What are you doing?!" she snapped at Poppy.

"Well the joke's over for that one!!" Poppy shouted clapping another bug between her hands. This time there was a tiny explosion of yellow sparkles.

"WHAT IS HAPPENING!!!!" Ella screamed. "I'm smooshing the laughing flies and their golden glow is exploding everywhere!"

Ella smacked Poppy on the arm, crunching another bug with a pop of light.

"I got another one!" Ella said excitedly, starting to enjoy the craziness that was happening.

The girls changed their strategy and started fighting back. There was a lot less laughter from the flying troublemakers and a series of luminous golden bursts of light as the girls chased the flies; which were not particularly fast, smacking and squishing them one by one. After several minutes of intense battle, the remainder of flying menaces realized they were losing and flew away. Poppy and Ella had won; and their golden glowing clothes, faces and hands were proof of their success. The girls were hysterically laughing as they watched the frightened and defeated flies retreat.

"That was *so* disgusting and *so* much fun!" Ella said grabbing Poppy's face between her hands, adding to the luminescence that was already there. "The boys will *never* believe us!"

"Nope!"

"Did you say nope?" Ella asked Poppy; but she clearly knew the answer since she was staring straight into Poppy's face and her mouth had not moved.

"It came from behind you," Poppy whispered.

Ella turned and looked ahead, where the path led into even more darkness. The girls, however, were shining so brightly that they didn't need a flashlight to see their immediate surroundings.

"I wish James was here. Do you think we should go on without him?"

"Nope!"

Poppy and Ella looked at each other doubtfully and then stared into the inky shadows before them.

"It looks like the path leads to a swampy area ahead, Pops," said Ella leaning forward, squinting her eyes.

"Let's wait for James. He'll know what to do," Poppy suggested hopefully.

"Nope!"

"Nope!"

"*WHO* is saying that?!" Ella shouted toward the direction of the deep voice. There was silence, except for the noise of the crickets and frogs in the swamp.

170

"Well, we can't just stand here. It's getting darker and I'm cold!"

"Yeah, I guess....me too, El. Maybe there's someone ahead who can help us. Everyone else we've met has been very nice."

"Nope!"

Poppy and Ella linked arms and walked along the path toward the sound of the voice. The further they walked the darker it became and the escalating chirps and croaks from the crickets and frogs filled the nighttime air. The trail disappeared into a murky swamp that blocked their way. They were both very glad they had suddenly become human flashlights, and they were able to find their footing in the gloom. Enormous ferns and exotic plants poked their heads from the depths of the water. Vines wrapped around spindly trees, tugging them toward the surface of the swamp water. The trees looked like old men bent over with aching backs. The tips of Poppy's sneakers were now wet with the sudden appearance of water and the disappearance of the path.

"Now what do we do?" Ella asked shrugging her shoulders.

"There must be a way to go around the swamp," Poppy said, searching the perimeter in the dim light.

"Nope!"

This time the voice was much louder and closer. It sounded like it was coming from the water.

"Who's out there?" Poppy asked a little timidly.

Silence

"We need to find a way across the swamp!" Ella shouted.

"Nope!"

"This is getting *very* irritating!" Ella shouted once again. "Can't you say *anything* besides nope?!"

"Nope!"

"Ahhh!" Ella growled clearly frustrated.

"Hold on," Poppy whispered to her, placing her finger against her lips.

"So, the only word you can say is nope?" Poppy said loudly, gazing toward the middle of the swamp where the voice seemed to come from.

Silence

"You must be *very* intelligent! You seem to have figured out how to cross the water!"

Silence

"We would be very lucky indeed to meet someone who is as smart and daring as you!"

There was a loud splashing sound and an *enormous* green frog with bulging black and yellow eyes vaulted through the air and landed at their feet. Their surprise guest shocked them so greatly that both girls fell backwards into the mud. Poppy and Ella propped themselves up on their elbows and stared into the rubbery wet frog face. He was gigantic; about 7 pounds, built like a cement block, about a foot wide and a foot tall. He blinked at them twice and squirmed a little bit closer to their feet.

"Hhhiii….my name's Pppoppy," she said a little shakily.

"Ella," was all that Ella could say.

Silence

"Do *you* have a name?" Poppy asked the giant green spotted frog.

He remained completely still, his bulging yellow eyes staring at the girls.

"Nope!" he bellowed.

"Oooooo…ummm……does that mean you don't have a name, or is your name Nope?"

"Don't be silly Pops! His name isn't Nope!" said Ella rolling her eyes.

"Yes, it is!" he yelped, his voice cracking.

The girls both suppressed a laugh at the change in his voice and because his name was apparently Nope!

"Why is your name Nope?" Poppy asked the frog.

"That's a dumb question Pops," Ella gave her a look. "Can you help us cross the swamp?" she asked, turning her attention back to Nope.

"Nope!

"Why do you want to cross?" He narrowed his eyes at them.

Poppy thought she could convince the frog to help them.

"We're trying to find the other Chatterbox Girl…. we've travelled pretty far already and we need to help her find her way home. We came to Chatterbox World and Firinne and James have helped us get this far, but we don't know where James is right now and……"

"Stop talking!" shouted Nope. "I don't like humans! They're noisy and destroy what is not theirs! There is no passage across this swamp!"

The frog remained silent for a whole minute. Poppy and Ella were not sure what to say.

"I see you've run into the Thug Bugs," the frog croaked, his googly eyes roaming over the glowing girls.

"We killed most of them and the others got scared off," Poppy said, making her most menacing face, trying to impress the frog.

"They'll be back. That was probably just a scouting party. Next time there will be many more and they'll bring Bully Bug for sure!" Nope warned the girls in his baritone voice.

"Who's Bully Bug?" Ella questioned Nope.

"He's their leader. You don't want to mess with him. He's tougher and bigger than any of the ones you ran into tonight and there's no such thing as surrender in his world. We have an understanding, he and I; he and his Thug Bugs keep the riff raff like you, away from my swamp and in return, my buddies and I don't eat him or any of his flashy army."

Poppy and Ella both looked worried. Bully Bug and the Thug Bugs were probably on their way back and Nope was definitely not going to let them cross the swamp. If only James was there to help them, they might have a chance. Nope Frog stared at the girls. They said nothing more, as they realized they were in a very tough position. Suddenly an idea popped into Ella's head.

"Well.... okay Pops," she said quite loudly, her eyes focused not on Poppy's face but on Nope's yellow protruding eyes. "I guess we have to go back and tell Gra that we can't help Mary because Nope Frog won't let us cross the swamp. We just don't have any other choice."

Poppy stared at Ella. She suddenly realized what Ella was doing. It was a brilliant plan. Gra was famous in these woods and Nope Frog would surely be scared of the grand owl who could kill him with one swoop over the swamp. She resisted the urge to hug her best friend; it was best to act out her part.

"He's going to be *very angry!*" Poppy said quite dramatically, adding a shiver to get her point across. "He told us to find Mary *no matter what,* and to tell him if anyone tried to stop us so......"

175

The two girls stood up and turned to make their way back.

"GRA!" croaked Nope Frog with a deep throated scream.

"Whyyyy you know him?" Ella coyly asked the clearly frightened frog.

"Uhhh maybe there's something I can do for you.... I mean you *do* seem better than the average humans....and you *did* thin out Bully Bug's army.... but then maybe the Thug Bugs were slacking off a bit.... I mean they let you two get through.... they're gonna have to answer to *me* for that...."

With a resounding bellow Nope Frog croaked for assistance, which came in the form of a passageway of turtle shells suddenly emerging from the depths of the swamp. With little time to spare before the return of Bully Bug and the Thug Bugs, Ella and Poppy scurried across the large oval shaped turtle backs, grabbing at the spindly tree branches for balance, disappearing across the swamp and away from the notorious negative frog.

CHAPTER 18

GRA ASKS FOR HELP

Finn, Charlie and Mike were having a completely different experience than Poppy and Ella, in Chatterbox World. They were not as amazed with their surroundings. They barely noticed the beauty around them. They were not greeted by James or Firinne and lead to the garden of roses. They didn't read the writing on the stone pillars. They never heard the tinker in the woods. They didn't stop in the vegetable garden they passed through for very long, since they had Mamo's sandwiches and French fries in their backpacks. They grabbed a few vegetables and jammed them into their packs for later. They were on a mission. They had to find Poppy and Ella.

Nothing was going to stand in their way. They all felt very responsible for the girls and they were very scared that something bad had happened to them. They were *extremely* afraid they would never see them again.

"You think we should split up and search for them?" Mike asked Finn.

"We don't know where we are or have any way to meet up again," answered Finn shaking his head.

"This is bad," Charlie said with a sigh, kicking the red dirt with his sneakers.

"We just keep following this path. They must have come this way." Finn sounded confident but was actually very worried.

They followed the same path that Poppy and Ella had taken before them. When they came to a fork in the trail; the one that Poppy and Ella had followed to the right, they decided to take the path leading to the left, down and around the edge of the mountain. The clay dirt became littered with golf ball sized rocks, that tripped and twisted the boys' feet. They grew weary and sweaty in the afternoon sun and welcomed the cooler temperature as day turned into twilight. They decided to camp on the edge of the woods. Unpacking their backpacks, they finished off the last remnants of Mamo's food and emptied the water from their thermoses. Mike rubbed his tired bleary eyes and wondered whether he was seeing things when he looked at Charlie, who was eating a carrot from the garden they had passed through that morning. He was about to make a sarcastic remark about Charlie's hair, which was beginning to take on an orange tinge, when a magnificent owl swooped over their heads and landed on a limb just over their camp.

It was Gra. Whisperings and gossip among the unseen creatures in Chatterbox World had brought him the news of the three boys travelling through the area. He needed to find out why they were here and what they were doing. By this time, Charlie had brilliant orange hair and Finn's fingernails were turning a deep green from the cucumber he was munching on, but they were too distracted to address their amazing transformations by the fact that an owl had just asked them a question.

"Hello there. My name is Gra. Who might you be?"

Charlie started violently choking on his carrot. Mike dug his fingers into his palms, very rattled that his friends were turning color *and* an owl was talking to them. Finn, who had started to accept that this place was totally different from where they had come from, although shaken, decided to answer Gra.

"We're looking for my sister Poppy and her friend Ella."

"Ahhh, well I think I can help you with that," Gra reassured the boys.

"You can!!??" shouted Charlie, casting aside the green leafy top of his last carrot.

Gra told the boys of his meeting with Poppy and Ella and he also told them about the mission he had sent them on to find Mary. He talked for more than an hour with the boys, telling them the story of Mary and Tim and how she came to be in Chatterbox World. They interrupted him to ask lots of questions, especially about the tinker. They were glad to know that it was his magical vegetable seeds that had caused them to become so colorful. They wanted to know if they could meet him.

"I'm sure you might. He has been keeping an eye on Mary," answered Gra.

"Where do you think Poppy and Ella are now?" Finn inquired when the grand owl finished his tale.

"I heard they had a little trouble crossing the swamps," Gra mused aloud. They seem to have escaped just in time to miss a battle between the Swamp Frogs and the Thug Bugs.

"The Swamp Frogs and Thug Bugs!!??" Mike squeaked.

"Yes, it seems Nope Frog felt that the Thug Bugs weren't holding up their end of the deal to keep everyone away from his precious swamp. It also seems that Poppy and Ella got the best of Nope and managed to find a way to pass through.

They must be very clever girls indeed! I heard that Nope Frog and his buddies ate more than a quarter of the Thug Bug army in retaliation and now their leader Bully Bug wants revenge."

The three boys stared at Gra, their mouths hanging open.

"I'm a little lost," said Finn.

"Poppy and Ella started a war!?" whooped Mike, who was thoroughly impressed with that thought.

Charlie grinned and nodded his approval.

"You'll have to be very careful passing through the swamps. Tensions are probably pretty high. Bully Bug will have his Thug Bugs watching the area and Nope is sure to block safe passage. You'll have to be as clever as your sister and her friend in order to make it through the area. I try not to get involved with the social interactions of the creatures of this world, things get too messy that way, but if you are in real trouble you can call for help and I will be there. Do any of you know how to whistle?"

"I do!" Finn said excitedly.

He demonstrated the two-fingered whistle his Uncle Ernie had taught him. The result was an intensely shrill eruption which startled the forest. Formerly unseen crows burst skyward, crying and alerting those below and the chirping of the crickets was silenced.

"Very impressive indeed!" Gra told Finn. "I will hear that from anywhere in these woods and come at once."

The boys put on their sweatshirts and laid on the woodland floor. They were tired and it was now completely dark, except for the light from the moon. Gra was deep in thought. He had closed his eyes and was concentrating; deciding, when his thoughts were interrupted by Charlie.

"Mr. Gra…. how are we supposed to help Mary get home when we don't know how to get back ourselves?"

"Don't worry Charlie. You'll just know what to do when the time comes. In fact, …." Gra started to say and then cocked his head to one side, fixing his large round eyes upon the boys. "In fact, I might have a proposition for you. I've got a gut feeling you boys might be just who I've been waiting for, to help me with a very tricky problem. Are you up for an adventure?"

This peaked the curiosity of Finn, Mike and Charlie. There was nothing they liked more than an adventure and impressing Gra would be awesome; for they definitely had to prove that they were even more clever than the girls…. that just needed to happen.

CHAPTER 19

TINKER TIDINGS

Poppy and Ella were very pleased with themselves and how they had tricked Nope Frog into letting them pass through the swamps. They giggled and talked about how frightened Nope had looked when they mentioned Gra's name. He had been wonderful and warm to them, but they could imagine the respect, mixed with fear, that the smaller woodland animals felt for the majestic large owl. Gra was the keeper of the stories of Chatterbox World, the overseer of all things happening, and more powerful than any creature they had met so far; well, except for Firinne.

"Your hair is still red and your eyes are green and you're still glowing a little," Poppy told Ella, suppressing a smile.

"OK, well *your* braids are tri-color, you have mud *all* over the back of your overalls, your t-shirt is ripped and your eyes are *much* bluer than usual!"

"Am I still glowing?" Poppy asked, trying to examine her arms and shoulders.

"I think you're down to 40 watts now!" Ella said with a laugh.

This started a giggle fest. Poppy and Ella laughed until tears were streaming down their faces. They were back on the trail. The sun was shining and it was a new day.

"James has been gone for a very long time," Poppy said over her shoulder to Ella, who was trailing behind, searching the landscape for something to eat.

"My stomach is grumbling again. We haven't eaten in *ages*!" Ella complained.

"At least there were a lot of berries in the woods. These fields are empty except for the wildflowers," said Poppy.

They had emerged from the forest early that morning. The red soil path had turned into a beaten down trail that led through a field of long green and yellow grasses. This field melded into

184

another, that was filled with thousands of towering sunflowers, all turned in the direction of the sun. It was hard to see more than a few feet ahead because the blooms were so high.

"I do love these flowers!" said Poppy peering up at the towering plants.

"Yeah, they make me feel very small!" said Ella twirling and tapping the giant stems with her fingertips.

Ella heard a noise behind her and quickly flipped around to see what it was. She was thrilled to see it was Firinne, plowing her way through the sunflowers.

"Firinne!" Ella shouted. The two girls ran to the beautiful spotted cheetah and hugged her sleek furry neck. The magnificent cat couldn't help herself and began to purr with happiness.

"You two look like you've been busy," she said eyeing the disheveled colorful girls.

"Yeah, we had a run in with the Thug Bugs," Poppy explained.

"I see," she said nodding her head. "The word around Chatterbox World is that you two can hold your own."

Ella and Poppy grinned at each other. This made them very proud.

"Firinne, do you know where we can find something to eat?" Poppy asked.

"And to drink! I can barely swallow!" Ella added.

"Why yes I do. Follow me."

Firinne left the trail and cut across the field of yellow and brown flowers. The girls followed closely, their stomachs rumbling. The sun shone brightly and the rainbow dragonflies delighted in what they found in the tall blossoms, but the girls grew so hungry and thirsty that they cared little for their surroundings. Poppy started wondering what the rainbow-colored bugs would taste like. She began to feel very grumpy and sweaty and tired. Ella thought it was taking a very long time to get to where they were going; but she also felt grateful that Firinne had appeared and was leading them to food and water.

"What *is* that smell!" Poppy blurted out crashing through the flowers and into a clearing, ahead of Firinne.

She stopped abruptly. Ella peeked over her shoulder. There he was; the tinker and his cart. His beautiful and muscular horse named Cob, was unhitched from the wagon and grazing in the tall grasses. The tinker held a large basket in his hand. The aroma coming from it was that of a freshly baked loaf of bread oozing with warm butter. He handed the basket to Poppy and smiled. Poppy and Ella smiled back. Firinne quietly settled down by the tinker's cart, intently watching the interaction between the tinker and the girls. Poppy and Ella stuffed the warm buttery bread into their mouths and washed it down with water the tinker offered to them from a tall silver cylinder. The water was cool and delicious; it tasted almost magical. After only a few sips, they were invigorated; their energy returned and they felt.... well.... just really happy.

Poppy loved being in the tinker's presence. She forgot that only a few minutes ago she had been hungry, thirsty and tired. Her thoughts were positive and she was filled with contentment. The world was okay. She was suddenly confident she would find Mary and that she would see Mamo and Seamus again. She missed Mamo. She missed everything about her; her hugs, her smile, her kind words, the feeling of safety and happiness she always felt in her presence and of course her amazing cooking. She wondered why she felt all these feelings so suddenly. The tinker handed each of the girls a canvas bag with shoulder straps.

"For your travels," he said searching Poppy's face. This time his smile appeared in his eyes as well as on his lips.

"Can I pat your horse?" Ella asked the tinker hopefully.

"Well you can certainly try," he answered, with the quickest of smiles.

While Ella delighted in stroking Cob's mane and whispering words of admiration to the impressive horse, the tinker turned his attention to Poppy.

"You are everything you should be."

"What do you mean?" Poppy asked returning his gaze.

"Smart, loyal, curious......but most of all you have a very kind and caring heart."

Poppy stared deeply into the dark brown eyes of the tinker. She wondered why he claimed to know her since they had just met. She inhaled sharply, catching her breath and holding it. Her eyes watered and her mind raced. She suddenly knew in her heart that she needed to find Mary; her life and everyone else's depended on it.

The tinker spread a large soft blanket on the grass for the girls to rest upon after they had eaten. He sat crossed legged on the blanket across from them.

"Gra told us the story of how you met Timothy and Mary," Ella said to the tinker.

"Gra is an exceptional storyteller. His account is true. He is very precise with his facts and does not stray from the truth or embellish his stories with unnecessary words. This is why he is essential to the balance of Chatterbox World. Other than myself, he is the only keeper of the past. He has collected the memories and history of Chatterbox World. The future of this world depends upon him too. I hear that Gra has his own serious issue of late, but that did not deter him from his responsibility of guiding you toward your very important undertaking. The task of finding Mary and leading her home is yours. No one can complete it but you. That doesn't mean that you are alone. You are surrounded by wonderful people.... like minds and hearts. The most intelligent people learn they need to work well with others. The most important thing is to make good decisions. Your success depends upon it."

"I have some questions that are bothering me," Poppy said.

"Ask away," replied Tinker.

"Welllll.... according to Gra's story of Mary and Timothy and how she got the chatterbox.... well, he said that was a very long time ago, long before I was born. How can she still be here? I'm confused."

"A very good question indeed. It proves you're a deep thinker. The answer is quite simple. Mary *did* come to Chatterbox World almost half a century ago. She stayed for only a brief time, that's to say, in *your* world's time, but in Chatterbox World, time doesn't matter. It is not in synchrony with the time in your world. You are here now, and she was here then, but those two time frames from your world, overlap in this one."

"So, I'm in her future and she's in my past, but we are here together since time overlaps and does not have the same meaning here, as it does in my world?"

"Yes! Exactly!"

"Well I guess it doesn't really matter, as long as we meet and I help her find her way home?"

"Right again!"

"My other question is: how will I know how to help Mary get home? I don't even know how *we're* getting home!"

"I cannot see that future. I have no idea what you will do to help her. Mary's heart is filled with great sadness. She is consumed by a fear of being left behind, of being alone, not needed, with no purpose in her life…. nothing to offer…. not necessary to anyone. Those are the thoughts that linger in her mind during the day and haunt her at night."

"How awful!" Ella said sadly.

"I couldn't imagine life without Mamo, Finn and Seamus….and you Ella," Poppy said, her eyes pooling with tears. We have so many people who love us…. like Uncle Ernie and Mr. Timpiste …."

"My mom and dad……and I'd even miss Charlie and Mike," Ella added.

"Uhhhhh……maaaaaybe," Poppy said starting to giggle; which of course erupted into another one of their giggle fests.

Tinker looked amused. The corners of his mouth twitched and there was a slight glint in his eyes.

Suddenly Poppy got serious.

"What if I make a mistake?"

"Mistakes are ok. That's how you learn what to do next time."

"Ok"

Poppy smiled; this time showing all her teeth.

The tinker smiled too; two of his teeth sparkled with gold.

"Mary sees things differently than you do .... I don't mean just because she is blind, but also because she is stuck in the present and fearful of her future; but you can bridge this gap and let her see that she has a very bright future indeed."

He paused, tilting his head to one side, studying Poppy's face.

"When you meet her, you will be tempted to give her Firinne's cheaters. You will want her to see the things you see and to make things easy for her. Firinne gave her the glasses when she arrived in Chatterbox World. Her response to seeing the world as we do was different than even I thought it would be. She was overwhelmed. They made her head ache. She preferred reading the pinned alphabet that Timothy had taught her, then the new foreign letters that we see. I'm not saying that she didn't enjoy seeing the world, but after I saw her response to wearing the cheaters, I realized it might be cruel for her to become dependent upon them and used to seeing, and then return to a world of darkness again. Do you understand what I am saying?"

"Yes, I do," Poppy nodded her head.

"I will leave the decision up to you. But I would suggest you give the cheaters to Mary only if you absolutely have to. Now, Cob and I need to be on our way."

The girls were sorry to say goodbye to Tinker and Cob.

"I'll miss you," Poppy said to Tinker as he started to pull away.

Cob stopped and the wagon came to a halt. Tinker looked over his shoulder at the two girls.

"Now that our paths have crossed, there's no need to miss me. From this day forward, no one will be able to take away the time we have spent together."

Firinne and the girls watched, as Cob pulled the tinker and his cart out of sight. Poppy and Ella stared at the horizon watching the clouds of red dust kicked up by the tinker's wagon, resettle on the ground.

"That's a lot to take in," sighed Ella, who had been quietly listening the whole time.

"Yeah it is," agreed Poppy.

"What's in the bags?" Firinne asked.

Poppy jumped. She had forgotten Firinne was there.

"Food and water!" Ella said excitedly.

The packs that Tinker had given to Poppy and Ella were filled with delicious looking wedges of cheese, more wonderful homemade bread, some fruits and veggies and more importantly, they each had a small version of the tinker's silver, water filled cylinder.

"The water from this funny metal bottle is so cool and delicious …I could drink a gallon of it!" Ella said.

"You want some Firinne?" asked Poppy.

"No thanks Poppy. I just had a long drink from the stream before we met…but thanks for asking."

Two ravens that were previously perched on the tinker's cart, were now circling the spotted cheetah cat, chattering and screeching at Firinne. The beautifully sleek feline rose and softly snarled at the noisy birds.

"We didn't get a chance to ask Tinker where we can find Mary!" Ella said, after slugging down some more of the deliciously refreshing water. "We still don't know where she is or what direction to go."

"Let's follow the tracks of Tinker's cart," Poppy suggested, dragging her feet along the wheel tracks in the red dirt.

They enjoyed a wedge of delicious cheese and some sweet purple grapes, which each of them found wrapped in cloth napkins inside their packs. The food and water re-energized them. No longer tired, feeling more refreshed than they had in days, the girls slung their canvas bags onto their backs and resumed their search for Mary. Ella paused and waited for Firinne to follow.

"Are you coming Firinne?" Ella asked the cheetah.

"I need to travel back to the other side of the forest," Firinne answered, as she turned her back to the girls. "The ravens are insisting that Gra is looking for me." With that comment, she slipped back into the tall sunflowers and disappeared from sight.

"You look normal again Pops."

"Yeah, your hair is the right color and you're not glowing anymore."

"Huh…. maybe it's the tinker's food and water. His vegetables are the reason we turned color in the first place!"

Poppy and Ella followed the wagon wheel tracks for close to a mile. The sun was high in the sky and the red dirt was dry and dusty under their feet. Except for the song of the red winged black bird and the occasional hum of the dragonflies' wings, the open prairie was quiet. Poppy was deep in thought about what she had seen in the tinker's eyes, and his comment about Mary not seeing the same things as she could. She wasn't sure what he meant about bridging the gap to Mary's future. Meanwhile, Ella hummed softly to herself, content and refreshed from Tinker's gift of lunch.

"Can you hear that?" Poppy stopped to listen.

Ella paused and closed her eyes, straining her ears. They could hear what sounded like the rumble of water.

"Maybe there's a river ahead! Let's go see!" Poppy shouted as she started to run.

Just over the next slope of land, was an enormous raging river, which disappeared over the edge of the mountain dropping 200 feet to the valley below. Ella tugged on Poppy's canvas pack and warned her to slow down. Digging the front of their sneakers into the grass embankment, they climbed the rocky side of the river and looked down the edge of the waterfall that plunged into what looked like a rock ravine below. Ella and Poppy lay flat on their stomachs on two giant boulders, peering over the edge. The roar of the falling water and the rainbow mist in the air around it was breathtaking.

"This is amazing!"

"Totally cool Pops!"

"How do we get down there?"

"Let's get back on the path and see if it leads to the bottom," suggested Ella.

She was right. The path did plunge down a steep hill and then around toward the right. It passed by the midpoint of the waterfall. The trail sloped downward and became very rocky and narrow. They were able to grab onto the few bushy branches that lined the descent. When the trail leveled out, Ella and Poppy stopped. Ahead of them in the clearing, about 50 yards away, sat a small log house with a flower and vegetable garden in front. From this distance, it looked like James and a girl about their age were sitting on the front porch.

CHAPTER 20

MARY MAKES SOME FRIENDS

They had found the other Chatterbox Girl and her name was indeed Mary. Ella and Poppy were very excited to meet her and to see James again too. Mary was ecstatic at the arrival of the two girls.

"I have so many questions to ask you!" Poppy said to Mary.

"James told me you were on your way here! I thought he was kidding!" Mary answered excitedly.

"I never kid," James said dryly.

"Come inside and we'll talk," Mary told the girls.

Mary seemed accustomed to the small log house. She stood up, revealing a flowered sundress in colors of blue and white. Her long, thick, dark brown hair hung in lose curls almost to her waist. Her light blue eyes were beautiful; however, her gaze was empty.

The inside of the house was very simple. There was only one room. In the center was a fireplace. A simple kitchen with a cast iron wood stove and a water pump attached to a stone sink was to the left, and a small single bed sat in the far side of the room. Above the bed was a loft with a log ladder leading up to it. Mary knew her way around the house as if she could see. She easily found the only chair in the room and took a seat in the old rocker. Ella and Poppy sat on the bed. Poppy got a sense that there was a close bond between Mary and James, when Mary instinctively dangled her hand over the side of the rocking chair searching for the touch of his fur. A fleeting smile appeared on her lips when her fingertips connected with his fluffy orange head. The three girls talked for more than an hour, filling each other in on the details of their time in Chatterbox World. Mary laughed out loud when they told her about the vegetable garden and how eating the veggies had changed their hair and eye color. She was also very impressed with their story of Nope Frog and the Thug Bugs.

"I would *love* to be part of an adventure like that!" she said excitedly, but then hung her head.

Poppy wondered what it would be like to be blind. Everything would be so different....so hard. Poppy thought to herself;

"The things that seem to matter; like how people dress, what color their hair is, the mean looks and whispers of others; these things are not actually important. What matters much more; like family and friends, being able to go to school and do things like other kids; these are the things that are really important and shouldn't be taken for granted."

Poppy and Ella had been careful not to mention all the details Gra had told them about Mary. They had agreed that it felt kind of like they were prying into Mary's private life.

"Would you like something to eat and drink? Perhaps a change of clothes? Tinker visits from time to time and brings me the most wonderful things. This little log house is so comfortable. There is always enough of everything; even the firewood never seems to run out!"

The night air was cooler, so Ella and Poppy made a small fire in the fireplace and in the cast iron stove, while Mary cut up some delicious looking fruit and vegetables, bread and cheese.

Mary went outside for a few minutes and returned with 6 eggs.

"You have chickens?" Poppy asked Mary.

"Yup! I have six chickens and a rooster in a little shed out back. You want some scrambled eggs?"

After dinner, Mary suggested they sit on the front porch for some fresh air and to watch and listen to the beautiful waterfall in the distance.

"It's called Geata Waterfall," said Mary, sensing the girls must be looking at the tremendous view of the falling water and the mountains behind.

Poppy reached for the cheaters and felt them in the front pocket of her overalls. She remembered what the tinker had told her about sharing the glasses with Mary.

"Wow! Look at all those stars!" Ella said pointing to the night sky.

"Poppy nudged Ella quietly shushing her, and then pointed to Mary."

"It's okay Poppy. I don't mind," said Mary."

Poppy wondered how Mary had heard her.

"I have extra good hearing," she laughed. I guess it makes up for my not being able to see. By the way…. can you hear that?"

"Hear what?" Ella asked.

"Listen very closely. Last night I heard a strange noise coming from the direction of the waterfall."

The girls listened intently.

All they could hear was the distant roar of the falling water.

James pushed open the screen door with his bulky forehead and joined them on the porch.

"I hear it too Mary. It's sounds like someone is screaming. I'll go investigate," he said.

"It might be dangerous James! And it's dark!"

"Mary, I'm a cat!" James said a little exasperated. "I'm pretty stealthy and I can see in the dark." He shook his head and disappeared into the night.

CHAPTER 21

GRA'S PROPOSITION

Gra definitely needed help. Although his thoughts were often consumed with all things past and present in Chatterbox World, his lifelong soul mate, a beautiful white and ivory feathered barn owl named Searc, was what he liked to think about the most. He could barely remember a time when he did not have her in his life. Her needs were a priority to him and his heart belonged to her. She had little to do with his life's work of overseeing Chatterbox World. She had *everything* to do with his peace of mind, his self-worth, his strength to lead and his determination to keep order; everything that shaped his outstanding character. Each night at dusk she would leave their nest and take flight over the sprawling prairies of Chatterbox World, floating on the air currents, enjoying the breeze between her feathers, searching below for their dinner. She was a master hunter with precision sight and hearing. No field mice in Chatterbox World were safe from her. She would return to their nest exhilarated, satiated and sleepy; with an evening snack for Gra. Upon her homecoming they would rest together and then he would take flight, soaking in the night air, checking in on the day's events with his contacts; who were spread far and wide across Chatterbox World. He would return to Searc well informed and tired. Toward the early morning hours, they would snuggle together in their nest, both loving the feeling of each other's warmth and comfort. A few nights before Gra met the boys however, was different from any other. Searc left for her twilight flight, but she had never returned. An aggressive thunder and lightning storm with torrential rains had moved into the area with great speed. Gra knew that this could be deadly for Searc, as owls cannot fly well in the rain. The storm was violent but also passed quickly. As soon as it was clear, he took off and flew faster than he had ever flown before; scanning the fields for hours into the deepest night. He flew as far as the magnificent Geata Waterfall that Searc adored. He started to panic at the thought that she might have lost flight over the pounding water. He searched until sunrise and would have searched longer had he not succumbed to the extreme fatigue that wracked his body. He returned to his nest to rest and regain his strength for a few daylight hours. He formulated a plan to reach out to all his contacts to watch for her, search for her, to put aside all other tasks and make this their priority. All the creatures of Chatterbox World knew Gra to be a kind and decent owl, but they also feared his power and strength and his notoriety for swift and deadly justice when necessary. Another night had passed and no one had seen Searc. He thought of a secret place that he and Searc liked to go to rest and rejuvenate. As far as he knew they were the only ones in Chatterbox World, other than the tinker, that knew it existed. It was a personal quiet spot for the tinker; where he rested from his journeys with his two ravens and his horse, Cob. Tinker had invited and welcomed Gra and Searc to his personal oasis. It was a place where they could meet to discuss important matters, and the owls could rest and renew their bodies and spirits. The entrance could be seen only from the sky. This made the meeting place even more discreet. Gra thought this might be a place where Searc had flown to escape the storm, as it was seldom affected by severe weather. It was surrounded by the mountain's rocky walls, which kept the wind and rain to a minimum. The location of the oasis was quite far from Searc's usual flight pattern, but he just had to check on the outside chance she had taken refuge there. On the other hand, he had heard whisperings of news concerning a loner, a feral cat named Eagla, known to all as a deviant who took pleasure in living in the rough and stealing for her own needs. She was a distant cousin of James. She was a vagrant, a roamer, who never settled down anywhere. Scrapping and stealing was how she survived. She made it clear that she didn't care that no one wanted her around. She was last sighted by a family of kit foxes who had left their grassland burrow to drink by the waterfall. Gra knew that Poppy and Ella were staying with Mary and that James had been spotted not far from that location.

His plan was to ask the boys to travel west and then north by land while he flew overhead in the same directions. They could search for any signs of Searc on the ground, while his sharp eyesight would unveil any clues by air. He would meet them at the hidden oasis, let the boys rest for the night, and then head east towards Geata Waterfall where they would meet up with the girls and hopefully, James. He knew there were caves under the waterfall that should be explored for any signs of Searc. He hoped in his heart that she wasn't there. He hated to think that she might be injured or trapped in the cold dark caves. There were creatures that took up residence in this underground world and he couldn't bear to think of Searc alone in their dark and dingy world. Gra told the boys that Firinne would meet them at Geata Waterfall and that the cheetah would gladly act as their muscle and guide. The owl thought this would be an excellent idea and the boys agreed. They had never seen a cheetah in real life before and were completely pumped to have one as a bodyguard in the caves. At sunrise, the boys headed north-west guided by the antique compass that Seamus had given Finn on his last birthday. Gra, contrary to his usual habits, took flight in the morning light and flew northwest as well. All who saw Gra in flight in the early daylight hours knew that Searc must still be missing and that this was serious business. The order of things depended upon Gra; and Gra was incomplete without Searc. Gra had dictated directions to Mike, who had drawn a map on the inside cover of the comic book he had stored in his back pack.

"Told you this would come in handy," he said to Charlie.

It was not a direct journey but a sweeping one to encompass the open plains to the west. He needed as much territory covered as possible and didn't want to omit any possible locations where Searc might be. Now that the boys knew that Poppy and Ella were safe, they were more comfortable with the detour Gra had proposed. Their first challenge was to cross the swamps under the watchful eye of Nope.

"He's tough and he's got lots of nasty followers who are willing to fight for him. My suggestion is to take the side of Bully Bug and the Thug Bugs and work together to finish off Nope and his slimy army," Gra advised. "If things get out of control and you need my help, give a whistle. In the mean time I'll head toward the open fields and start my search. I'll keep watch for you. Hopefully you'll make it to the plains in a day or two."

The boys were excited for the challenge. Not one of them would admit that they were also a little scared.

CHAPTER 22

A BARGAIN WITH BULLY BUG

It was mid-day when Finn, Charlie and Mike reached the edge of the swamp; the same place that Ella and Poppy had encountered Nope. It looked less foreboding in the daylight since the sun's rays filtered through the sagging trees. There was no apparent way to cross the mucky water, so they decided to leave the path and skirt the edge of the swamp to the right. They did not get very far, when Charlie, who had taken the lead, started to sink into the mud, which almost sucked his sneakers off his feet. Finn and Mike pulled on

Charlie and just managed to back out of the mud themselves.

"This isn't gonna work," Finn told Charlie and Mike. "We need to find another way to get across the water."

"Ahhhh!" shouted Mike as he flipped in a circle and smacked himself in the head.

Charlie started hysterically laughing at Mike, but this ended abruptly when a Thug Bug smashed head on into his right eye.

"Creepers! I'm blind!" he screamed jumping up and down holding his hands over his eye.

Hundreds of Thug Bugs descended on the three boys with force, smashing into them biting and laughing. Finn and Mike started to run, wildly swinging their arms trying to fend off the massive biting bugs, while Charlie rolled on the ground screaming with each attack, protecting his swelling eye with his fist.

"Bully Bug! Bully Bug! We come in peace with a bargain from Gra! Bully Bug! Bully Bug! Listen to us! We want to make a deal!" shouted Finn, now crouching on the ground trying to protect his face from the assaulting insects.

Suddenly the Thug Bugs stopped attacking. They hovered in the air above the boys. Their laughter had ceased and the only noise remaining was that of their whirring wings. As quickly as they had appeared, they suddenly disappeared into the trees. The boys stood up. They were covered in bites that began to swell and itch. Charlie tried to open his eye, but it was now swollen shut.

"What's the deal?" they heard a small voice ask.

The boys searched, looking in all directions for the owner of the voice.

"I'm over here on the rock."

Finn, who was hurt the least, staggered over to a huge boulder nearby. On the top sat an enormous Thug Bug the size of a golf ball; easily twice the size of the other Thug Bugs.

"Are you Bully Bug?" Finn asked.

"I am," answered the bug. He glared at Finn with his bulging black eyes.

"We need to cross the swamp. We want to make a deal with you to fight Nope and his army; to get rid of them for good so you can live in peace and reclaim your land. We are willing to help you if we can obtain safe passage across the swamp in return."

Bully Bug scrutinized Finn. He then looked at Charlie's blotchy red swollen face. He scowled doubtfully at Mike who was scratching at the red bumps that covered his arms and neck. Luckily the boys had long pants on.

"How are *you* going to help *me*? It doesn't look like you can even defend yourselves! ….. never mind help me!" Bully Bug snapped at the boys.

"I…. I have an idea!" Charlie pushed past Finn, walking toward Bully Bug.

"I'm listening," Bully Bug answered. "*What's the difference,*" he thought. "*If I don't like the plan, I'll recall my army and finish off these useless humans.*"

CHAPTER 23

CHARLIE'S PLAN

S everal hours later, when the daylight faded and the deafening chorus of bullfrogs started their racket, the boys began phase one of Charlie's plan. They had spent the last two hours gathering small dried deadwood from the forest floor. They stacked as much as they could find in a large pile by the edge of the swamp. Finn's assignment was to find three thick sturdy sticks that could be used as clubs. It was a challenging task and he could find only two that would do the job. Then they collected all the small rocks they could find. They looked for anything they could carry that was baseball sized or a little smaller. They made a circle about three feet in diameter, composed of the largest rocks they could carry. Mike dug out the center of the circle using a found piece of deadwood that resembled a claw. They filled the center of the hole with dried leaves and twigs. Charlie, who was a decorated boy scout, was proud of his ability to make an ember with whatever he could find in the woods. Before long, the little pile of leaves was smoking.

Charlie added a few more twigs and the driest pieces of wood they had collected. With the first crackle of fire, they heard exactly what they were hoping to hear.

"Nope!"

"Nope!"

"Nope!"

Nope frog was roaring at them with his usual comment. He sprung from the swamp with such force that he slammed against the front of Mike, knocking him over. The boys were astounded at the immense size of the frog.

"Nope!"

"You will NOT have a fire by my swamp! You will NOT!" the irate frog screamed at them.

Mike shoved the frog aside, jumped to his feet and joined Charlie and Finn. He scooped up a toaster sized rock and held it over his head. The three boys stood their ground, glaring down at the giant frog, pursing their lips and squinting their eyes for effect.

"I could crush you with one blow from this rock!" shouted Mike.

"Go ahead and try it and you will have the *full* force of my army upon you!" shouted Nope.

This was just the challenge that the boys had hoped for. Mike raised the rock high over Nope's head.

Nope screamed, "Attack! Attack! Crush them! Bite them! Drag them into the swamp!"

The festering pool came alive with an army of frogs, huntsman spiders and slithering snakes. They swarmed the boys, smothering their fire. The snakes hissed, snarled and snapped their fangs. The frogs jumped, croaked and tried to overwhelm them with their numbers. The spiders looked for an exposed arm or leg to bite. But Nope's scream of attack, not only summoned his army, but it was the call that Bully Bug and the Thug Bugs had been waiting for. They had never had the ability nor the opportunity in the past, to draw *all* of Nope's Army from the depths of the swamp at once. This was their chance to bring Nope and his entire army down for good. The Thug Bugs outnumbered Nope and his slippery army by far. The turtles, who were never willing participants in Nope's devious plans, remained in the water, secretly hoping the tyrant would be killed in the fight. Their once peaceful swamp had become an awful place and they were ready to take it back. Mike and Charlie braced themselves against the gang of frogs that lunged at them, with their slimy rubbery bodies. It was quite a disgusting feeling, but the surge of adrenaline helped them to keep control. They were armed with the bulky sticks that Finn had found and Charlie and Mike used them like golf clubs smacking the attacking frogs, flinging them into the air, squashing them against the trees. With a wild swing, Charlie smacked one of the largest frogs in mid- jump. It exploded all over Charlie's face adding to his wretched appearance. Mike howled with laughter. Finn used the rocks they had gathered, launching them at the slithering hissing snakes while thick clouds of Thug Bugs bit into their skin. Bully Bug was intent on taking down Nope Frog. He buzzed around the giant frog's head trying to attack from behind to avoid Nope's long reaching sticky and very deadly tongue. Bully knew that if Nope was able to grab him with his tacky weapon, it was all over. He would be swallowed in one gulp. The boys and the Thug Bugs were dominating the fight. There were only a few snakes and spiders left to deal with and Mike and Charlie seemed to be in control. Finn knew that it was time for the final phase of Charlie's plan. He dropped to his hands and knees and crawled quietly toward the edge of the swamp, positioning himself behind Nope. Bully Bug taunted and buzzed over Nope's head, being careful to stay just out of reach of his dreaded tongue. Finn watched for Bully Bug's signal. Bully's eyes bulged and he puffed up his body making a deafening buzzing sound. At this very moment, Finn grabbed Nope by his hind legs and pulled. Nope panicked and tried to break free. Taking advantage of the fact that Nope was distracted, Bully Bug slammed into Nope's bulging eyes, blinding him with his phosphorescent light. Finn twisted and threw his back pack onto the ground, grabbed Nope by the middle and stuffed the blind, screaming frog into the pack. It was a very tight fit and Finn needed Mike's help to get the zipper fully closed. The few remnants of Nope's army slithered, hopped or scurried into the depths of the forest, hopefully never to be heard from again.

The boys shouted and celebrated their victory with high fives, shaking their fists in the air and punching each other on the arm. Bully Bug had lost some of his Thug Bugs in the battle, but their victory was sweet and the heroes had died for a worthy cause. The swamp and its surrounding woods were now free and Nope was a prisoner in Finn's backpack. Bully Bug landed on Charlie's shoulder. Mike and Finn came close.

"I am forever in your debt," Bully Bug told them. "I never *dreamed* that three human boys would help me take back our woods and our swamp. You are a credit to your race. As long as you are in Chatterbox World the Thug Bugs will be with you in times of need and you are always welcome to our protection."

Charlie, Mike and Finn felt like they were on top of the world. Gra would be *so* proud of them and more importantly, Mike thought, *"they had definitely outshined the girls."*

CHAPTER 24

THE TINKER'S OASIS

After the battle, Finn, Charlie and Mike had crossed the swamp on the back of the turtles, much like Poppy and Ella had done before them. They had camped on the edge of the forest and slept soundly under the careful watch and guard of the Thug Bugs. Nope had remained very quiet in Finn's backpack. He hoped they would forget he was there so he could escape as soon as one of them opened the pack. The next morning, they said farewell to Bully Bug and the Thug Bugs and headed northwest in hopes of meeting up with

Gra. They soon found themselves on a flat, raised, tree lined path. It was long and straight and to either side the woods dropped off at an almost vertical slope. They walked closely together, careful not to wander toward the edges. About a half mile in, the path opened into a clearing and led up a steep incline to the left. Finn led the way scrambling up the hill, jumping onto a leveled-out surface at the top. He was followed by Mike and then Charlie. They continued this path, which slowly became more of a tunnel as the trees got closer together and more bent, forming a dome topped roof overhead. They lost sight of the forest behind them and grew weary of the cool dim light of the heavily canopied trail. They longed for the warmth of the sun on their backs. Their Thug Bug bites still stung and itched, and the scratches and bruises they had acquired during the battle were sore. Charlie's eye was still closed and little pieces of frog guts were stuck to the sides of his face. Mike and Finn didn't look much better. Finn was tired from carrying the heavy frog in his backpack. He didn't feel badly for him since there were holes in his pack that were designed for drainage in rainy conditions. He was sure that Nope had enough air to breathe. He squeezed the bulge of the hateful frog against the canvas pack. Nope jumped and shouted.

"Nope!"

Mike smirked and said, "Wait 'til we hand him over to Gra! He'll surely be yelling Nope when that happens!"

This comment filled Nope with dread. He squashed himself down to the bottom of the bag and remained quiet as a mouse.

Finn saw a glimmer of sunlight ahead. This motivated the boys to pick up their pace. They broke through the edge of the canopied pathway into the bright sunshine of a grassy cliff. The sight of the open valley below with its rolling green velvet grass took their breath away. A herd of wild horses grazed on the opposite side of the open field, far away from the boys, but they had already been noticed. A murder of crows had been disturbed by their emergence from the woods. They flew over the open fields, cawing and shouting to everyone within earshot, the arrival of Mike, Charlie and Finn. The boys bolted down the steep hillside running full tilt, shouting and laughing.

"We made it!" Mike shouted.

"Look at those horses!" Finn pointed to the now galloping herd.

"I wanna ride one!" Charlie shouted enthusiastically.

"You can't do that you nutjob! They're wild horses!" Mike laughed at Charlie.

"Look! It's Gra!" Finn shouted, pointing up at the owl circling over them in the sky.

They broke into a run and headed to the west side of the open field where Gra had disappeared into a cluster of trees. By the time they reached the small gathering of ash trees they were out of breath. Charlie dropped to the ground heaving his back pack to one side and laid on his back. Mike and Finn did the same.

"It's good to see you boys!" Gra said from the branch of a giant ash.

"It's good to see you too Gra!" they answered.

"We fought with the Thug Bugs and beat Nope's army!" Charlie said puffing up with pride.

"O no! I forgot Nope was in my back pack!" Finn held back a laugh, realizing he had just hurled Nope through the air, ending with a crash on the ground.

"I heard about your victory. What an accomplishment!" said Gra.

"Ahhhh, did you say that Nope is in your back pack?!"

Even though Nope was a terrible tyrant, Finn felt a *little* badly that he had just launched his backpack so roughly onto the ground. He cautiously unzipped the bag and peered inside, hoping the nasty frog was ok. Before he had time to react, Nope sprung from the bag and took off through the grassy field, hopping at an amazingly high speed.

"Oh no! He'll get away!" shouted Mike jumping up and running after the frog.

Gra laughed a deep throated laugh that the boys had not heard before.

"Come back Mike. No worries for you. I'll give him a sporting head start!"

Mike dropped to the ground where he was and all three boys waited to see what Gra would do. A light wind ruffled his feathers and he pecked at an itch under his left wing. He looked very relaxed and unconcerned that Nope was now out of sight.

"We shouldn't let him get too…" Charlie started to say, but at that moment, Gra took flight and in a blink of an eye he plummeted toward the ground and then rose back up into the air with Nope dangling from his beak. They could hear Nope screaming.

"Nope! Nope! Nope! Nope! PUT ME DOWN!!!"

Gra disappeared over the eastern ridge of the mountains that rimmed the other side of the valley, leaving the boys alone in the quiet, lying in the soft green grass, admiring the magnificent horses galloping in the distance. They wondered aloud to each other what would become of Nope the Frog, but they agreed that Gra would do what was best. It was some time before Gra returned to the boys.

He said nothing of Nope's fate and they didn't dare ask.

"You must be tired and thirsty," he said. "Follow me. I will show you a place you can rest before we head east to meet up with your friends."

They followed Gra's lead to the edge of the mountain on the west side of the valley, and slipped through a crack in the face of the rock that was not visible until they were upon it. They entered a long oval oasis bordered on all sides by the mountain. It was a secret wonderland. The air was instantly cool and fresh. Visually, it was a lot to take in. In the center, was an ancient wisteria tree with lavender blossoms that hung like an oversized umbrella. Lilac bushes in full blooms of white, pink and purple edged the rock wall on one side. A sliver of a waterfall, only two-foot-wide, plummeted down the rock face and gathered in small pools. The thick green bushes to the left of the boys had been trimmed and shaped into giant three-foot ravens; others, into oversized turtles. Charlie made a face at Mike and Finn.

"Is this place for real?" Charlie said to no one in particular.

"It's *very* real," came an answer from behind one of the turtle bushes.

Finn, who was closest to the greenery, jumped. The tinker, who had been bent over trimming the toes of the farthest turtle, now stood and faced the three boys, pruning shears in hand. He gazed at them with a curious look upon his face. Mike and Charlie grinned at the tinker. Finn suddenly noticed the tinker's cart parked on the far side of the garden. Cob was lying on his side next to the cart breathing deeply, apparently enjoying a deep slumber. Both of Tinker's ravens flew toward the boys and perched themselves on top of their look-alike bushes, joining in on the staring-fest.

"Whoa! I think it's the ..."

"The tinker!" said Finn interrupting Charlie.

"That I am!" Tinker said with a smile that was so fleeting that it could have easily been missed. But the boys noticed and were glad of that brief smile.

"We're….um…. we're looking…. I mean we're looking…."

"For Searc," Mike finished Charlie's sentence.

"That's very kind of you," said Tinker. "I am sure that Gra appreciates it very much. Most of Chatterbox World is looking for Searc right now. It's a shame she is missing. Would you care for something to eat? Perhaps a drink of water?"

"Yes please!" the boys answered together.

"Thank you, Tinker," said Gra. "The boys have had quite a journey and they need rest and nourishment."

"I can see that," said the tinker inspecting Charlie's swollen eye and the bites and scratches on the boys. "Come drink from the water; I believe it will make you feel better."

The cool clear water that fell from the mountainside and pooled amidst the soft green grass and scattered wildflowers was indeed the most delicious and thirst-quenching water they had ever ingested. Charlie's eye began to heal and their bug bites and scratches disappeared. Their sore muscles no longer ached.

"We've heard great stories about you Mr. Tinker," said Charlie. "Like how you gave the chatterbox to Mary."

"Yes, Charlie," replied Tinker with a twinkle in his eye. "It was actually Timothy that gave the chatterbox to Mary, but of course I did play my part. I've heard good stories about you three boys as well."

Charlie's eyes widened. He was very happy that the tinker had heard of them. Charlie rubbed his eyes and yawned. It was contagious. Finn and Mike yawned as well, staring bleary eyed at the gathering of black crows that were forming on the tips of the greenery.

"Take a moment to rest under the wisteria tree," suggested Tinker.

A quick minute after they sprawled on the grass under the fragrant shady tree, all three boys were fast asleep dreaming of the incredible things they had experienced in Chatterbox World. Little did they know their adventures had just begun.

CHAPTER 25

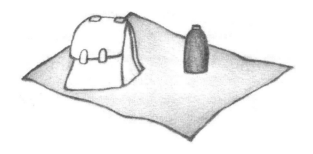

KOKO LAKIKI AND JIBBERJABBER

Charlie, Mike and Finn woke more than 12 hours later to the caws of the black crows and the brilliance of the late morning sun. They felt refreshed and very much alive, ready to head east to finally meet up with Poppy and Ella. The girls were weighing heavy upon Finn's mind and he wasn't that pleased to have been diverted to search for Searc. At the same time however, he wanted to help Gra, and he was very grateful for the rest and refreshments and the chance to meet the tinker. Tinker gave each of the boys a pack of food and water, similar to those he had given to Poppy and Ella; but these also included a thin woven blanket.

They thanked him, patted his horse, Cob, and bid him farewell.

"If you are in need of my help, just look for one of my ravens or their cousins, the crows. They will keep me informed of your progress."

Gra said his farewells to Tinker and Cob, nodding to the ravens who watched their every move with their dark eyes; and then they were gone, disappearing through the crack in the rock ledge, keeping a quick pace as they traveled east across the open plain.

They left the galloping wild horses behind and disappeared into a forest green with pine and cedar trees, welcoming the coolness of the woods after walking more than a mile across the open fields. They had lost sight of Gra, who flew ahead to scan the trees for his beloved Searc. Finn suggested they stop for a quick rest and a drink of water from their silver thermoses.

"This water is magical. Not only did it heal all our wounds but it makes me feel ...I don't know ...great!" said Charlie.

Mike and Finn nodded in agreement, drinking deeply from their apparently bottomless water coolers.

"I can't imagine how long we've been gone," Mike said in between swigs of water.

"I don't like to even think about it," said Finn. "Mamo and Seamus must be crazy worried about us. I'll be glad to meet up with Poppy and Ella again."

"How we supposed to find our way home?" asked Charlie.

"Well, we have to help Gra find Searc first," Finn said shaking his head.

"What's that over there?" Mike whispered pointing in the direction of a huge pine tree.

Although they knew the woods were filled with creatures, most of them had managed to stay out of sight.

"I don't see any ..." Charlie started to say and then he froze. He *did* see something. It looked like a shadow. It made his heart race a little.

Finn stood up and walked toward the giant tree. The shadow disappeared. Charlie and Mike joined Finn and they inspected the area. They saw nothing.

"Must have been just a trick of the light," said Finn. "Let's get going."

They trudged on through the pine and cedar forest taking deep breaths of the cool aromatic air, making very little sound on the carpeted pine needle floor. Charlie glanced over his shoulder. He was a little spooked. He saw it again. Or at least he thought he did; a glimpse of a shadow ducking behind one of the lumbering pines.

"I just saw it again; behind us," he hissed in Mike's ear.

Mike flipped around, searching, listening. Finn did the same.

"Cut it out you two! You're freaking out about nothing. Now you got *me* looking over my shoulder!" snapped Finn.

The boys picked up their pace and headed due east, trying not to think about what might be following them. They didn't feel like talking; they were busy thinking their own thoughts. Then suddenly what they had decided was just a trick of the light, or a shadow cast by the towering trees, was now standing in front of them in plain sight. The three boys stopped in their tracks. Only the call of a chickadee singing its little heart out somewhere above in the canopy, broke the stillness that prevailed between the boys and the creature that blocked their path. It was almost indescribable. So different from anything they had ever seen before, but at the same time, very much like them. It was a boy, well at least it looked like one, with the most beautiful skin they had ever seen; like milk chocolate, but richer and creamier. His eyes were a deep emerald green. He was about Charlie's height, but *very* slim; bendable like he was made of clay. His arms and legs were long and spindly. His body swayed slightly, appearing to have no joints, or even bones. He was hairless, smooth, very curvy; his movements were quick but graceful.

"Are you looking for Searc?" it asked in a very smooth soft voice that drifted through the silence.

They didn't answer. They just stared. Charlie felt his knees begin to quiver.

"Yeah, we're helping Gra," Finn answered, without taking his eyes off this unusual creature.

"Who are you?" Mike asked mustering up his toughest voice, the one he used at school to intimidate.

"I'm Koko. Koko Lakiki," he answered, curling up the corners of his lipless mouth into a very dramatic smile. His face resembled the yellow smiley face that was popular back home.

"Are you made of ......of rubber?" Charlie asked feeling more courageous, taking a few steps toward Koko.

"Chocolate," Koko answered matter-of-factly.

"Coooooool!" Mike and Charlie answered together, totally impressed and amazed and not really believing it was true.

Koko walked right up to Finn and peered at him closely, only inches from Finn's nose. Finn gazed wide eyed at the stunning creamy fluid-like skin and the oversized deep green eyes.

"You don't even look *real!*" Charlie said reaching out to touch Koko's long spindly arm.

Koko turned his smile towards Charlie and Mike. His whole being shifted slightly and regained its shape again in a split second. They were looking at a person made of chocolate, in a form somewhere between liquid and solid. It was the strangest most wonderful thing they had ever seen.

"I'm helping Gra too. Mostly everyone is. No one seems to have seen Searc after the intense storm the other night. Gra has spread the word that you are welcome guests in Chatterbox World. May I join you? I would love to hear stories about your world. My best friend is a human. His name is Jibberjabber."

Koko walked with Charlie, Finn and Mike, asking them question after question about where they had come from and where they were going. Koko listened intently to the boys' stories. He especially liked to hear about the battle between Nope and the Thug Bugs. Koko laughed and laughed holding his sides and then suddenly ran up the closest tree trunk, did a back flip and then landed on his feet beside Charlie.

"That was CRAZY!!!" Charlie shrieked.

"You're AWESOME!" Mike shouted.

Finn shook his head in disbelief. *Chatterbox World is certainly full of surprises!*" he thought.

Koko enjoyed entertaining the boys while they continued on their way. He was quick and agile and seemed to be able to do incredible things with his flexible body. He bounced from tree to tree, ricocheting off the bark, adding a flip or cartwheel in between.

"Where's your human friend, Jibberjabber?" asked Finn, remembering Koko's earlier comment.

"He went ahead to search for Searc on the border of Pernicious Woods."

"What's Pernicious Woods?" Finn asked Koko.

"A place you don't want to be; where someone like Nope Frog would be hunted and eaten as a snack by evil creatures and those who have lost their way."

"Oooooooo," Charlie said shaking his head no, signaling Finn that he had no interest in going there.

"We could handle it," Mike said crossing his arms over his puffed-up chest, nodding his head, looking very confident.

"Well Jibbs is going to check with our contact on the border. Hopefully they'll be no need to venture into the woods." Koko reassured Charlie.

Charlie sighed deeply, and the mood became more solemn. Within the next half hour, they came to a fork in the path. To the left, the path plunged downward. The trees became gnarled; choked with climbing vines. The path to the right was lined with tall cedar trees and looked less foreboding.

"This is where we part ways," Koko said with a smile and wink. "I will check with Jibbs to see if he's discovered any news about Searc. I'll follow your trail and meet up with you again if you like."

"Sounds like a good plan," answered Finn.

"Do you need our help in the Pernicious Woods?" asked Mike.

Charlie dug his elbow into Mike's side. He didn't want anything to do with Pernicious Woods.

"Nah, we'll be okay," Koko said poking Mike in the side, copying Charlie's gesture. "Sounds like you have enough on your plate as it is."

Mike opened his mouth to argue but it was in vain. Koko did a double forward flip, bounced onto a cedar tree, ricocheted off another and disappeared out of site down the dark and gloomy trail to the Pernicious Woods.

"That guy is mega cool!" Charlie said to Mike. "Why did you offer to go to Pernicious Woods with him? You trying to get us killed?!"

"I wonder if that's where Gra took Nope," Finn said looking at his friends.

"It would serve him right if he did," Mike answered.

"Koko is seriously *the* coolest kid I ever did see though," Charlie said wide eyed. "Did you see the way he changed shape and the super flips he did!"

"You couldn't do *one* summersault if you tried," laughed Mike. "That guy is the opposite of you. You've got like one joint in your body and you use it to eat."

"Okay Muggins, shut your trap! You're no gymnast yourself!"

"Let's get going," said Finn shaking his head with a laugh. "You two are clowns."

They followed the rest of the path through the towering cedar trees, spotted with the occasional pine, and then stopped to ask any woodland creatures they saw if they had seen or heard anything about Searc's location. They would occasionally hear the caw of the crows from above. It gave them a little comfort knowing they had a way to send a message to Gra or the tinker if need be. The path began a descent into a thin ravine and they thought they could hear the rushing sound of water below. As they emerged from the woods and out into the open ravine, they came upon a winding river only about 10 feet wide. The water gushed and swirled, picking up momentum as it plunged even further down the rocky slip. Since there was no sign of rain or wind, they decided to camp by the water for the night. They unrolled their blankets and Charlie built a campfire. They snacked on the delicious food that the tinker had supplied for them. The packs containing food were truly magical in that they never seemed to empty, and their water supply did not diminish no matter how much they drank. As the light began to fade, they talked about Koko and what his friend Jibberjabber might be like. Koko had said that Jibberjabber was a human. They wondered why he was in Chatterbox World and how he got there.

"I can hear someone coming," Finn said shushing Mike and Charlie.

They remained still and quiet, focusing their attention toward the sound of the voices. It was Koko and someone else, probably Jibberjabber, approaching them from a totally different direction than they had entered the ravine. Koko seemed to glide through the low bush blueberries. Jibberjabber, who was tall and well built, plowed through them stomping and crushing the branches as he went. They stopped a few yards away from Finn.

"Hi I'm Finn."

Jibberjabber glanced at Finn, and then at Charlie and Mike. He said nothing. He was tall, good looking and muscular with a terrible scar that ran across the right side of his face, just missing one of his deep blue eyes. His hair was shoulder length and ragged and there were visible old scars on his arms. For a boy probably only a few years older than Finn, Mike and Charlie, he looked as though he had been through some tough times.

"You can call him Jibbs. I do. I think he likes it better. You do ...don't you Jibbs?"

"Yeah," he said looking at Koko with no emotion. "Be back."

Jibbs took off running in the direction of the river. He ripped off his tattered t-shirt and jeans right down to his boxers and jumped into an isolated small pool that had gathered between two large rocks. He soaked himself up to his chest, closing his eyes and tilting his head back, breathing deeply.

"He loves water. It seems to calm him," Koko said to the three boys.

"He doesn't talk much?" Charlie asked.

"He knows enough to get by. Talking is not important to him. He's the smartest, sweetest and toughest kid you're ever going to meet. He doesn't like to be touched and he doesn't trust anybody; well let's just say he is very discerning and you need to prove to him you are trustworthy."

"How long has he been in Chatterbox World?" asked Finn.

"As long as I have. We came together."

"It's kind of a long story; but the basics are simple. His parents and pretty much everyone else didn't understand him; why he can't speak and express himself, why he gets upset easily, doesn't like to be touched. His parents thought he was stupid and disobedient, so they punished him and eventually gave up on him. They were the owners of a candy store. They would lock him in the back room during the day. They couldn't send him to school and they were embarrassed of him. I'm pretty sure I'm a figment of his imagination; a friend to keep him company. I love him with all my heart and would protect him with my life and he would do the same for me. I think he did a wonderful job creating me in his imagination. I am very happy with who I am."

"How did you two get to Chatterbox World?" asked Mike.

Koko glanced at each of the boys, widened his eyes, took a breath and began:

"Well.....one day after closing the candy store, his parents left together to run an errand. They had forgotten to lock the door to the back room. Jibbs and I decided to make a run for it. We never looked back. We lived on the streets for a good long while. We survived through some tough times and encountered some very mean people. One rainy, chilly night, we huddled together under a large refrigerator box that we were lucky enough to find. We had discovered it in a dumpster and set it up out of sight at the end of an alley. The sound of the rain was comforting as it pelted the box over our heads. We were so happy to be dry, especially since I don't do well in the rain. That was when we heard something approaching. It was the

tinker. He appeared out of nowhere. We peeked through a tear in the box and thought we were dreaming, but he was real. The tinker smiled at us. He wasn't angry or mean. His smile was something new to Jibbs, who was used to angry faces. This smile made him happy. The tinker held out his hand. Jibbs usually trusted no one, but he cast our cardboard box aside and took the tinker's hand. Tinker looked at me. Now that was a first; no one had ever seen **me** *before, other than Jibbs. I rested my hand on theirs and our whole life changed. We were here; in Chatterbox World. It was a beautiful sunny day. Our troubles were over. For the first time in our lives we were free; warm, dry, our bellies full with the food and drink the tinker shared with us. We had fun running through the fields, travelling miles and miles with Tinker and Cob. We were given the gift of peace and happiness. Now don't get me wrong. All of Chatterbox World is not rainbows and butterflies.*

239

There is darkness and evil here, just like other worlds.
I'm not worried about Jibbs though. He learned how
to be tough while on the streets; how to fight and
survive. Lacking in courage he is not."

Koko sighed a deep sigh and gazed over at Jibbs.

"The one thing that he loves second to me is water," he said with a light laugh.

"Why is he called Jibberjabber?" Finn asked gazing at Jibbs, who had left the water and was redressing.

"That's what his parents called him. They could never understand what he was trying to say. The few words that he could speak came out rapidly so they cruelly nicknamed him Jibberjabber."

Charlie's eyes teared up and Mike stared at the ground and bit his lip. Finn's heart ached in his chest and a lump formed in his throat. He thought about his life and all the love he had been given. He made a mental note that if he ever made it back home, he would never take anything for granted. He would be more accepting of others. It was at this moment, Charlie, Finn and Mike became better people, with a clearer understanding that every person faces their own unique challenges in life; and some are dealt far more difficulties than others. Their eyes were opened to the fact that *all* people are different and do not need to fit into the mold of "normal" to be accepted and treated with respect.

Jibbs returned to the fireside and plopped down, holding his hands out toward the warmth. His t-shirt and jeans were damp, so Charlie offered him his blanket. He took it and smiled at Charlie.

"Did you forget your shoes by the river?" Mike asked Jibbs.

"No shoes." Jibbs answered shaking his head.

"He doesn't need shoes," Koko said with a smile. "His feet are as tough as leather. By the way, I think I'll move away from the campfire and sleep over there, a little closer to the river. I don't want you to wake up in a puddle of melted chocolate."

CHAPTER 26

THUG BUG BELLIES

When Finn opened his eyes the next morning, he saw a sight that warmed his heart. Jibbs was sitting crossed legged by the riverside. He was stroking Gra's feathery head and singing quietly to the owl. Finn joined the pair and sat beside them.

"Gra," said Jibbs.

"Yes," Finn answered with a warm smile. "Hi Gra. Have you seen any signs of Searc?"

"No," Gra answered sadly.

"Searc!" Jibbs shouted excitedly, pointing to the East.

"There!" Jibbs jumped to his feet with his arm stretched still pointing east.

"Have you heard something?!" Gra sputtered, flapping his wings in midair.

Jibbs shook his head yes.

"Where? Who told you?" Gra questioned Jibbs excitedly.

"Pernicious Woods," said Jibbs with a very serious look in his eyes.

"You went into Pernicious Woods!!!" Gra raised his voice. "I know you and Tinker have dealings in there, but I'm not happy about it. I cringe every time I think of the danger you encounter."

"Go help Searc! Koko comes!" Jibbs gestured for Koko to follow.

Jibbs started to run east, away from the group.

"Wait!" Gra shouted. "You should all travel together. Do you know exactly where she is?"

"Searc! Giant Geata Waterfall! In caves! Come!"

"Thank you Jibbs! Thank you! YOU DEAR WONDERFUL GUY!" Gra bellowed as he took flight and disappeared in the distant eastern sky.

"Wonderful guy!" Jibbs said with a toothy smile.

"You're the BEST!" Mike said slapping Jibbs on the back; then he froze. They all froze. Jibbs peered at Mike, studying his face. He grinned an even brighter, wider smile and slapped Mike hard on the back. Jibbs was very strong, Mike was almost knocked off his feet.

243

"Wonderful guy!" he enthusiastically said to Mike.

Everyone laughed including Jibbs. Koko did three back flips and just barely avoided landing in the smoldering fire pit; which made everyone laugh even more.

"We better head out," Finn said packing up his bag. The others did the same. They threw dirt on the smoldering fire until it was completely out and headed in the direction that Gra had flown.

"According to my compass we're travelling dead east," Finn said over his shoulder to the group.

They hiked for about two hours and then stopped to rest and take a drink. Charlie offered water to Jibbs but he declined, taking a tiny cylinder from his jeans pocket. It was a miniature version of the ones that Tinker had given to them. It didn't look possible that much water could exist in the tiny container, but Jibbs took a long swig and smiled at Charlie, apparently thirsty no more. A large, sleek, black, velvety raven appeared in the sky overhead and landed on Jibbs' shoulder. He squawked and did a tiny dance down Jibbs' arm and squawked some more. Jibbs stared at the raven sitting on his outstretched arm. Then he nodded his head and the Raven took to the sky and disappeared.

"What did he say? Could you understand him?" Finn asked Jibbs.

"Come! Poppy!" Jibbs said, pointing up the sizable hill in front of them.

"Poppy?!" shouted Mike, Finn and Charlie all together.

"Poppy! Come!" Jibbs nodded.

It took almost half an hour to climb the enormous hill. Jibbs was in excellent shape and got to the top a few minutes before the others. Koko did a combination of running, flipping and bouncing up the hillside. When they got to the top they were greatly rewarded. They could see the massive Geata Waterfall in the distance.

"Probably one day's trek away, maybe a little more," said Finn shading his eyes.

There was a sea of green leafy tree tops below that stood between them and the march to the waterfall. One more walk through the woods and they would be a few hours away from Poppy. The vision of the Geata Waterfall spurred them on. They tore down the incline that lead to the forest entrance and surged on without a care or concern. Koko obviously arrived at the bottom first. He flipped and flopped down the hillside and then bounced up again to wait for Jibbs. They gathered together on the edge of the woods before them. Now, both of tinker's ravens descended upon them from the sky, squawking louder than ever. Both ravens flew back and forth between the boys screaming a warning:

245

"Go around! Go around!" they screamed at the hiking party.

"Are they saying what I think they're saying?" asked Charlie.

"They don't want us to go into the woods," Mike said.

"It'll take *ages* to go around though," said Finn.

They all looked at Finn.

"You want *me* to make the decision?" Finn said incredulously. He thought for a moment. "Look, there's five of us. What could possibly be in there that we can't handle?"

Charlie peered into the gloom of the forest before them. He shook his head uneasily.

"Bring it on!" said Mike with confidence.

"Bring it on!" Jibbs echoed.

"We got this!" added Koko.

"Alright, alright," Finn said, putting up his hands in surrender and then scratching his head to think. "I have a feeling we should listen to the ravens, but if you all think we should forge ahead then let's do it!"

Upon entering the cooler air of the forest, they tightened their ranks and moved swiftly together. This section of woods had a faint beaten path, probably made by the migration of animals. They encountered more than one fallen tree that blocked their way, but they worked together and managed to pass through. The deeper into the forest they walked, the cooler and damper it became. The former smell of fresh air and pine morphed into a musty aroma of dead vegetation. The trees were laden with oppressively wild and tangled vines. The forest was eerily quiet but now and then they heard the scream from an animal somewhere deep in the woods. Charlie's stomach was beginning to really rumble for food but he didn't want to suggest stopping. Something about these woods made him feel very uneasy.

"We must be about half the way through," said Finn. Let's stop for a few minutes to rest and then make a push to get to the other side."

The party of hikers were glad for the rest. They had been walking all day and their feet were aching and their hopes of making it to the waterfall by nightfall were now dashed. Finn knew that dusk was quickly approaching, and he didn't want to camp overnight in this forest. He was struggling to hide his uneasy feelings and lead with a positive vibe. Perched on the remains of a large fallen tree, Charlie, Mike and Finn offered some food to Koko and Jibbs. Jibbs gladly took some but Koko refused. They were all deep in thought, chewing on bits of fruit and bread, so they didn't notice what was happening around them until it was too late. The vines in the surrounding trees had slowly crept down toward the boys, encircling them and twining themselves together to form a wall. Jibbs noticed it first.

"Run!" he shouted.

The only one that could have made it out in time was Koko and he refused to leave Jibbs' side. They were trapped in a web of vines that was growing thicker by the second. It was blocking their view of the surrounding woods and even more startling; the light. Within twenty seconds they were entombed in the web of greenery. Charlie began to panic and smash his fists against the wall of vines. Koko jumped from one side to the other attempting to smash his way free. Finn grabbed his treasured jackknife from his pack and tried hacking at the vines. Each time he stabbed at them, a shrill scream emitted from the plant and it would immediately begin to tighten and reinforce the hole he had started.

"Oh boy," Finn said breathing hard, his mind racing with ideas on how to get out of this predicament.

"Charlie!" he said breathlessly.

"Charlie, can you find anything to make a fire with?"

"Yeah…. maybe, but that's not going to help. We take the chance of going up in flames *with* the vines."

"There's got to be another way out," said Mike.

Jibbs was on the ground slowly rocking back and forth. His eyes were closed, his hands were clamped around his knees, fingers laced, holding them closely to his chest.

"He'll be ok. He's just escaping from the scene to think of solutions," Koko told the boys with a weak smile.

A slender bit of vine detached itself from the outer wall and slipped into the belt loops of Jibbs' jeans. It coiled itself through the loop and started to travel around his waist. In the flash of an eye Koko snatched the vine and ripped it from Jibbs, shredding the greenery from the stem as he attacked.

Jibbs jumped up and crossed to the other side of their tangled cage, but another vine from the other side immediately tried to loop around his ankles. Then the real trouble started. The menacing vines began attaching themselves to each of the boys. Luckily Koko was too quick and slippery for them to successfully grab hold of his chocolate body. He continued to fight off and detach each of the vines attacking the boys, but he was outnumbered, and the vines began to win the fight. Charlie, Finn, Jibbs and Mike continuously ran, darting in a new direction each time to avoid capture. Charlie was the first to go down. His ankles were bound together and he tripped. Another vine took advantage of the situation and grabbed hold of his right arm. Koko tried to release the toppled Charlie but the vines wouldn't budge. Mike was next, then Finn. Koko decided he could protect only one of them and it was going to be Jibbs. He wrapped his flexible chocolate body around his friend so completely that Jibbs now looked like he was made of chocolate. The idea worked. The vines could not attach themselves to Jibbs' new slippery skin. Charlie began to scream for help. Mike and Finn joined in. It had all happened so quickly that Finn had forgotten to whistle for Gra's help. Finn's legs were bound but his arms were still free. He jammed his thumb and index finger into his mouth, inhaled as deeply as he could, and emitted the loudest, shrillest whistle of his life. They hoped the crows or Tinker's ravens would hear Finn's whistle and their calls for help. Something needed to happen and soon, because Finn now no longer had the use of his fingers, arms or legs. He was wound up tightly, not unlike a mummy, and his breathing was becoming more labored by the minute.

"I think we're gonners," gasped Charlie.

"I think I'm gonna pass out," Mike said, with what little breathe he still had.

"I think I hear something," Finn said weakly.

"Caw, caw caw!"

The boys' fear and exhaustion changed to hope and excitement when they heard the screams of not a few crows, but an army of crows shrieking and squawking and cawing. The crows threw themselves at the interwoven tenacious vines, pecking and clawing with their beaks and talons. The cage began to quiver as if in pain, but as quickly as the crows tore into it, the vines would pull tighter, repairing the holes. A few of the crows' feet were becoming entwined as well. Then came the most welcome sound; a sound that Mike, Charlie and Finn knew well. It was the glorious drone of thousands of Thug Bug wings. They stung and bit into the vines with such ferociousness that the plant began to howl and release its grip. The crows shredded what was left and the vine released its hold and began to untwine itself and shrink back to the heights of the upper tree branches. It hissed and moaned and screeched and recoiled until they were all free. Koko unwrapped himself from Jibbs, who then looked up into the night sky with wonderment. The phosphorous bellies of thousands of Thug Bugs composing Bully Bug's army, lit up the forest, chattering with laughter and cheers for their success. Not one Thug Bug was injured, and they had saved their allies.

Bully Bug flew directly to Finn and sat on the end of his nose. Mike howled with laughter. They all laughed at the sight of the giant golf ball sized bug camping out on the tip of Finn's nose. Jibbs approached Bully Bug and held out his palm. Bully took flight and landed right in the middle of Jibbs' outstretched hand. He brought the bug close to his face and smiled the happiest of all smiles.

"Wonderful Bug!" Jibbs' cheered.

The night air filled with laughter. The crows cawed and the Thug Bugs joined in on the fun by diving and swarming, filling the darkness with what looked like a thousand shooting stars.

"We shouldn't lollygag!" roared Bully Bug, interrupting the noise.

"Time to leave! Time to leave!" screamed the crows.

The grateful travelers gathered their things and followed the massive swarming light of Thug Bug bellies. It guided them through the forest and back out into the open night air. They could wait no longer. They urged the Thug Bugs to continue leading them through the night to reunite them with Poppy, Ella and Gra.

CHAPTER 27

A CHAIN OF EVENTS

The days that Mary spent with Poppy and Ella, were some of the happiest in Mary's young life. The three girls went on walks and picked flowers from the fields, to make bouquets for the house and fragrant crowns for their hair. Their favorite activity was picnicking near the waterfall. Poppy and Ella were glad they were in the habit of wearing their bathing suits under their clothes during the summer. They never knew when they would get a chance for a swim in the river or a dip in the lake. On the warmest of days, they swam in the small pool near the rocky edge, being careful not to float too close to the powerful churning waves, where the falling water mingled with an array of giant boulders. Poppy and Ella helped Mary onto a large flat rock on the side of the pool. It was a great place for Mary to dangle her feet into the water. She still felt uneasy about being near the edge, since she had fallen into a river when she was little. Her fingers clutched the little hand carved chicken she kept in her sundress pocket. She rubbed her fingertips over the smooth surface of the wood, smiling as she remembered Timothy's words to her, when he gave her a replacement for the one she had lost.

"The first chicken I carved for you was not *really* a chicken at all," Timothy had said to Mary.

"Why do you say that?"

"Well he wasn't much of a chicken if he dove into the water and swam away! He must have desired to be a fish and I just didn't know," Timothy said very seriously.

This made Mary laugh.

"I'm pretty sure *this one* is a real chicken," Timothy said, his heart lifting because he had made her happy. "Let me know though, if it wanders off and disappears like a cat or pinches your skin like a bee, and I'll try again."

"You're silly," Mary said out loud.

"What did you say?" Poppy asked, hoisting herself out of the water and plopping down on the rock next to Mary.

"Oh…. Nothing," she said with a smile. "I was just remembering…."

"Hey you want to go check out the lower part of the waterfall?" Ella asked joining them on the rock, dripping water all over Mary's dress.

"Yeah! Let's change and go exploring!"

"I don't know…" Mary said nervously.

"It's ok. We'll link arms! We can take our time!" Poppy said excitedly.

"It will be fun!" agreed Ella.

"I'll just slow you down," Mary said shaking her head.

"It won't be any fun without you!" Ella scooched down next to Mary and took her hand.

"Yeah we're a team!"

Other than Timothy, Mary had never had close friends before, especially two girls her own age, and she had certainly never been part of a team.

"Okay!" she said shaking with excitement.

James crawled out from under a nearby bush and stretched his orange striped body as far as it could extend. He yawned and used his back foot to scratch behind one ear.

"You know…. that's where the screams were coming from the other night," he said shaking a bit of leaf from his ear. "The water falls into a rocky ravine at the bottom and covers the mouth of a large cave like a curtain. I decided to wait for Firinne to return before I ventured too far into the cave. You never know what might be lurking in there. I sent a crow to check on Firinne and to ask if she would meet us here."

"We saw Firinne on our way here," Ella told James. "She said the ravens told her that Gra needed help with something. That was a few days ago."

"Hmmm, something must be going on," said James.

By the time Mary, Ella, Poppy and James made their way down to the very bottom of the waterfall, it was late afternoon.

"It sure is loud!" Mary shouted over the pounding of the water into the plunge pool at it base.

"There's a narrow rock ledge that curves behind the water. You can't see it from here because the waterfall is blocking our view, but behind it is the entrance to the cave." James shouted to the girls. "I think we should wait for Firinne. I'm surprised she hasn't joined us by now. There must be something serious going on with Gra."

They waited for about an hour, hoping that Firinne would show up. The girls laid on their backs on a grassy almost vertical slope that overlooked the gathering pool. It was easier to talk at this distance away from the roar of the water. It felt nice to soak up the sun and laze about in the grass. Poppy couldn't stop thinking about everyone at home, and how they must be frantically looking for her and Ella.

"How long have we been gone?" she wondered.

Time seemed to pass very differently here. She remembered what the tinker had told her about time in Chatterbox World and how it had no relation to the time back home. It was weird to think that Mary was from her past and that she and Ella were from Mary's future. It was all so confusing that she decided not to think about it anymore. It didn't really matter anyway. Some days seemed longer than others. They had met Mary only a short time ago, but somehow it felt like they had known her forever. There was no awkwardness when they met. Their personalities just clicked.

"Do you miss home?" Mary asked Poppy.

Poppy's focus turned back to her surroundings. "Yeah, I miss Mamo the most I think."

"Who's Mamo?"

"She's my grandma ...the best in the whole world. I can't imagine life without her ...she ...and Ella, of course ...are my best friends."

"I have a best friend," Mary said quietly, her eyes pooling with tears. "But he's moving away. I might never see him again. *What am I going to do without him?"*

Mary began to sob uncontrollably.

Poppy and Ella put their arms around Mary and hugged her, not sure what to say. Mary's sobs quieted down and she sighed deeply.

"Well *we're* your friends now!" Poppy jumped up and tugged on Mary's arm, helping her to her feet.

"Yeah! Everything's more fun with you around!" Ella grabbed Mary's other hand.

Mary smiled. She was feeling very glad and very lucky to have not one, but two new friends. They made her feel happy and ...normal. They didn't seem to mind that she was blind. They didn't treat her like she was made of glass; unable to do the things they were doing. She felt freer than she had ever felt before.

Firinne never met them at the waterfall that afternoon but when they awoke the next morning, they found the spotted cheetah lounging on the front porch in the morning sunlight.

"Firinne!" the girls shouted, excited to be with their friend again.

They each took turns hugging the charming cheetah. While Ella absent mindedly massaged Firinne's shoulders with her fingers and scratched behind her ears, Poppy and Mary told the spotted cheetah about the screams they had heard the last two nights. They told the story together, finishing each other's sentences. Firinne grew very concerned that the screams were somehow related to Searc, but she kept her worries to herself. She would talk to James about it later. James watched Firinne and the girls from inside the house, peering through the screen door. He marveled at how the girls had become close friends and how much happier Mary seemed to be. She no longer cried in her bed. Each night, the three girls chattered and giggled until they fell into a contented sleep. Sometimes it made his ears ring they talked so much, and Mary began to join in on Poppy and Ella's giggle fests; but James' heart swelled with happiness for Mary.

James joined them on the front porch, just in time to hear Firinne say that she had news from Gra. She told them all about Searc and how she had disappeared. James and Firinne exchanged worried looks. They were both thinking the same thing; that the cries for help they had heard coming from the waterfall might have something to do with Searc.

"On a happier note," Firinne continued, "Finn, Charlie and Mike are on their way to meet us!"

"WHAT!!!!!" shouted Poppy and Ella together.

"YOU MEAN THEY'RE IN CHATTERBOX WORLD!!!!" Poppy shrieked, jumping off the porch.

"Apparently so!" Firinne answered, amused at Poppy and Ella's reaction. "They've been helping Gra look for Searc in the West. The most recent crow told me that they should arrive here today. We shouldn't waste any time once they are here. We will go into the caves together and look for Searc."

Poppy's mind raced. She was so shocked that the boys were in Chatterbox World and that they were working with Gra. She and Ella were very happy with the news. They had told Mary all about the boys, so she was eager to meet up with them as well.

"I can't wait to see them and hear what they've been doing!" said Ella.

"I think they've been busy," Firinne said with a smile. "I've heard rumors that Nope Frog's army was overthrown by the Thug Bugs and that your friends were involved."

"Good riddance to that wart faced tyrant!" James said with a smirk.

The girls slipped into the cabin and changed out of the night clothes that the tinker had kindly given to them. Poppy slipped her overalls on over her bathing suit. Ella dressed in jeans, a belt and a borrowed cotton shirt from Mary. Mary wore her flowered sun dress. It was a warm sunny day and they were all excited about Firinne's plan to search the caves. Mary's nerves had been replaced by excitement; especially with the arrival of Firinne and the news that she was going to meet Poppy and Ella's friends. They waited on the porch with Firinne and James, scanning the horizon for any signs of Finn, Mike and Charlie. It was mid-morning when Poppy spotted movement in the distance. She couldn't make out what it was. It looked like a swift moving rain cloud heading their way, but there were no other clouds in the sky so that didn't make sense.

"Look El! Do you see that dark cloud?" Poppy said pointing west.

"Yeah what *is* that?" she said shading her eyes from the sun. It looks like there are people coming too. Maybe it's Finn and the guys!"

It *was* Finn and the guys and the closer they got to the log house, the more excited everyone got. The dark cloud began to funnel and then disappeared back over the mountain. They could see five people coming toward them now. Poppy decided she couldn't wait any longer and took off running in the direction of the visitors. Firinne decided to join her in case there was trouble. Ella grabbed Mary by the hand and they took off after Firinne, James following closely behind. Poppy flew into Finn's arms and hugged him, wiping tears of happiness from her face. Charlie and Mike both smacked Poppy and Ella on their backs, trying not to show how excited they were to see them. Charlie turned red in the face when Poppy grabbed his arm and gave him a huge bear hug and a kiss on the cheek. Mike put his hands up in defense and backed away from the girls, laughing. Ella grabbed Finn's hand and squeezed it tightly, telling Finn that she was truly glad to see him and his dopey friends. Poppy introduced the boys to Mary. Mary took each one of them by the hand and said "nice to meet you" with a big smile that she hoped they would like. During the excitement of the reuniting friends, Jibbs and Koko sat on the grass some distance away from everyone else. Mike quickly explained that Jibbs and Koko were friends of theirs and that Jibbs had led them in the right direction; that he was the reason they had found their way to Poppy and Ella. Both girls were shocked at the unusual appearance of Koko but waved and smiled at him and Jibbs. Koko waved back but Jibbs just stood and said "Come!" There was much excitement, and they all talked at once while following Jibbs and James back to the log house. Everyone was trying to fill each other in, sharing stories of the things that had happened to them since they arrived in Chatterbox World.

"Sorry to interrupt!" said James in a loud voice.

The group quieted down and looked at the orange tiger cat.

"We need to check out the caves and look for Searc without any more delay."

Everyone agreed. Finn was happy that they had stopped and slept for a few hours in the early morning, guarded by the Thug Bugs. They dropped their packs in the log house and combined what they needed into one backpack, which Mike volunteered to carry. Finn grabbed a very stout hickory walking stick that was propped against the fieldstone fireplace. He thought it might come in handy.

"Has anyone heard from Gra?" asked Finn.

"Yes, I have," answered Firinne. I left him early this morning down by the entrance to the caves. He told me he would wait there for us. He didn't want to leave, in case he heard or saw any signs of Searc.

"Stay here," Jibbs told Koko, motioning toward the log house.

Everyone was surprised and looked curiously at Koko, who peered unhappily at Jibbs, shaking his head no.

"Stay here!" Jibbs told Koko more firmly this time.

"Why don't you want him to come?" asked Charlie.

"Jibbs loves water, but water doesn't like me," said Koko sadly. "He imagined me to be made of chocolate and so chocolate is what I am made of. I think Jibbs is afraid I'll turn into chocolate mousse!" Koko said with a weak smile.

Charlie muffled a laugh. Mike shoved him so hard that Charlie almost lost his balance.

"Well we really could use a scout at home base here; someone to send a crow to the tinker if we don't come back by...... let's say......midnight. Would you do that for us Koko? It would be an important part of our mission." James smiled encouragingly.

Koko's demeanor instantly changed from sad to happy.

"You'll take care of Jibbs?" he asked shifting his eyes from one person to another.

"I think Jibbs is going to be the one to take care of *us*!" Finn told Koko with a smile. "He's one tough guy!"

"Wonderful guy!" agreed Jibbs with a big smile.

Firinne and James led the way, but as soon as they approached the waterfall, Jibbs scrambled down the rocky slope and disappeared behind the falling water. Poppy and Ella each took one of Mary's hands and guided her to the meeting spot behind the roaring cascade. The spray from Geata Waterfall soaked them all. They were very glad they had left Koko behind, and were delighted to see that Gra was perched on a rocky ledge patiently waiting for them. After a quick hello to Gra, they decided that Firinne would enter the cave first.

"Mary should stay here while we go into the caves." Finn suggested.

Mary's head dropped, and she looked both disappointed and worried.

Poppy's mind flashed back to the tinker's warning about the cheaters; but then she confidently made a quick decision.

"I have a better idea," said Poppy removing the cheaters from the bib pocket of her overalls. She tapped the back of Mary's hand.

"Mary, take theses glasses and put them on." Poppy helped Mary loop the glasses around her ears. Mary's face instantly lit up with a smile.

"You all look so wonderful! Where did you find Firinne's cheaters? I lost them a while back…."

"No time for that now!" said Firinne.

"Mike, would you mind if I hitched a ride on your backpack?" asked Gra.

"Works for me!" Mike answered with a smile. He was actually very proud that Gra had asked to travel with him instead of someone else.

Gra flew to the rugged canvas backpack and dug his talons into the fabric.

"Let's go!" James bellowed.

They were now a party of ten. The deeper they moved into the cave, the more the light dimmed. They followed a wide tunnel down and around to the right. Although they were travelling downward, the tunnel made so many turns, they were no longer sure which direction they were moving in. It got narrower as they went and before long they had to walk single file. Firinne led the group, followed by Jibbs and Mike. Jibbs was very impressed with Firinne and every time he was close enough, he stroked the cat's beautiful sleek fur. The noise from the waterfall lessened for a while, but then increased as they walked deeper into the base of the caves. At its narrowest point the rock walls offered a small space, just big enough to squeeze through. Mike was extra careful because of his precious hitchhiker. Each of them edged their way into the large expanse of a beautiful cavern. The ceiling had a gaping hole, formed by the relentless pounding of water over many years. The waterfall plunged through the opening and crashed into a rushing river, that snaked its way through the cave in a very deep wide gorge.

"I thought we had moved away from the waterfall, but it seems we've ended up where we started only much deeper. I wonder how much further down these caves go! Do you know how deep they are Gra? What does this water empty into?" asked Finn.

"I don't really know," answered the owl. "I've never ventured down here."

Gra released his grip on Mike's backpack and flew over the water filled gorge, searching for Searc in the cracks and crevices of the giant cavern, but his progress was hindered by the ceiling which plunged sharply down, forming a rocky arch that hung over the flowing water. There was no way he could pass by this area without getting his wings soaked from the spray and he couldn't get enough height to fly.

"Looks like you'll have to try and squeeze through with me on your backpack," Gra said to Mike.

"I have a better idea," answered Firinne. "Rather than take a chance of getting injured or falling into the water, why don't you stay here and listen for Searc in case we are headed in the wrong direction. We don't even know if she passed through this way. Chances are slim that she made it through this low archway."

Even though Gra knew that Firinne was right, he really didn't want to be left behind. After thinking for a moment, he told Firinne to move ahead without him. They reassured Gra that they would do everything in their power to find Searc and lead her to safety.

Mary shook with fear, overwhelmed by the sights around her and the rushing water, but the thrill of being part of the rescue party was a stronger emotion. She glanced back and forth between everyone's faces, intrigued with their facial expressions and what they looked like. She reminded herself to focus on the job at hand. She didn't want to be different; she wanted to be a useful member of the group. Being able to see was a little disorienting. She was used to doing things in the dark, feeling her way, listening; but nothing was going to stop her from keeping up with the others. The party of nine pressed on. They each squeezed under the rocky arch, their legs and feet getting soaked by the river water lapping the tiny ledge on either side. They followed the water deeper down into another branch of caves. The light from the outside world diminished and then disappeared. Firinne and James could see well enough in the dark, while the others used the flashlights they had stored in Mike's backpack. Of course, Mary didn't mind the darkness at all; the cheaters allowed her to see the room a little more clearly than the others. She was having trouble concentrating however, since the thoughts and emotions of everyone around her swirled in the air, somehow visible to her. She blocked this out as best as she could and concentrated on her footing. They surprised some unsuspecting bats who took flight, avoiding their unwelcome visitors. Mary paused and inhaled sharply. She spotted a chameleon clinging to the wall, intently glaring at them. She wasn't sure *what* he was, but she didn't like the look in his eyes. Poppy squeezed Mary's petite hand tightly when they heard a loud screaming noise that echoed throughout the cave.

"That's a cat," said James quietly to the group.

Again, the loud screaming resumed, this time repeating itself over and again, echoing off the walls.

"Silence!" shouted Firinne.

Her command surprised the group since no one had ever heard Firinne raise her voice before. Her demand bounced off the cave walls, asking for silence three more times. The screaming stopped. They waited.

"Searc?!" She called out a little more delicately.

Nothing.

"Searc?!" Firinne shouted with just a tinge of fear in her voice.

"Searc?!" she repeated, this time a little more hopefully. The sound of her voice echoed throughout the dark underground world.

"Firinne?"

A weak and scratchy sounding voice called out the cheetah's name.

"Where are you?" Firinne called out, tilting her head to one side, straining every muscle to locate where the sound was coming from.

The screaming and howling began again and the proprietor of it appeared, eerily illuminated by the light of their combined flashlights. They gazed upon a large framed, black and grey striped, bone thin cat. Her fur was matted and thin. Her eyes were gaunt. She looked desperate and fearful. She screamed and moaned, pacing back and forth. She was directly across from them, about 15 feet away, but on the other side of the turbulent water.

"That's Eagla!" said James.

"I'd recognize that dirty scoundrel anywhere!" Firinne growled.

"Now wait, come on," James said to Firinne. "She's not a bad cat! Everyone's too tough on her. She's just had a rough time with life; has trouble fitting in. She looks half starved. Let's just see what she has to say."

"What are you doing in here! Where is Searc?" Firinne shouted over the noise of the water.

Eagla stared intently at them from afar. Her dirty thin face surrounded two large sunken eyes. Her fur was matted and damp. She *did* look very forlorn. She made a noise that was somewhere between a meow and a scream.

"Answer Firinne!" James shouted. "Where is Searc?!"

"She is here! came a scratchy weak reply, which they could barely hear over the rumble of the water.

"Where is she? I don't see her?" asked Firinne.

"She crawled inside the back of the cave behind me. It's a very cramped space. I don't think any one of you could get in there ...well maybe that small girl there," she said motioning toward Mary with her paw. Her voice was very hoarse. She didn't look well.

"I'll go in and get her!" volunteered Mary enthusiastically.

"How you going to get across the water?" Charlie said half aloud.

"It depends how deep it is," said Firinne.

"The water's rushing pretty fast. We have to make sure she isn't swept away in the current," added Mike.

Before they had a chance to stop him, Jibbs darted over to the water's edge and flipped backwards onto his stomach, crawling like a crab down to the rushing water. Firinne scrambled down the rocky embankment and grabbed hold of Jibbs' shirtsleeve just in time.

"No!" shouted Jibbs. He wriggled away from Firinne and slipped into the water. Jibbs' legs were extremely muscular and he took to the current with great ease. Jibbs was the tallest in the group; Firinne was relieved to see the water level reached only to the bottom of Jibbs' thighs. Jibbs plowed his way across to the other side directly below

Eagla. He faced the intensely forceful water and planted his feet far apart.

"Mike! Come!" he shouted motioning with his left arm.

"I know what he's doing. I know what his plan is. What a smart guy!" Firinne shouted to Jibbs.

"What's the plan!" James shouted over the noise of the water. "We can't leave him out there! He'll get swept away!"

"We're going to make a chain. Everyone put your flashlights on the rock ledge to illuminate the river. Mike, you make your way to Jibbs. Finn, you still have that walking staff?"

Finn searched around the cave floor and found the sturdy staff he had cast aside.

"Mike, use the staff for support. Stick it securely into the rock bed under the water. When you know it's wedged in there tightly, slowly make your way across and grab Jibbs. Finn, grab hold of Mike's belt and Charlie hang on to Finn's. Once you reach Jibbs, pass the staff to the next person. Ella, you follow next and then Poppy. I'll stay back and shine one of the flashlights on you! Hurry now! Plant your feet carefully! As soon as you get in place, link your arms as tightly as you can!"

Mike lowered himself down into the gorge. Finn followed and then Charlie. Finn grasped Mike's leather belt so tightly his knuckles were white. Charlie wildly hummed "Bridge Over Troubled

Waters" while clutching Finn's belt. They entered the water together; Mike digging into the rocky bottom, bracing himself with the formidable hickory stick. Finn planted his feet and leaned away from the current, but Charlie slipped and crashed into the water. Poppy screamed and slid over the edge, scraping her hands and knees. Ella followed and grabbed Poppy by the back of her overalls. Charlie's tightened grip on Finn's belt was all that kept him from being swept away. He regained his footing and tightly linked arms with Finn. With his free left hand, Charlie held the long walking stick toward Ella. The weight of the hickory was too heavy to hold one handed and the end of the stick dipped into the water. Firinne dropped the flashlight from her mouth resting it on the edge of the ravine, pointing the beam toward them as best as she could. She crashed into the river and grabbed the end of the stick with her teeth, treading water and straining her neck to raise it above the surface. Charlie held his side of the hickory pole with all the strength he could muster in one arm and steadied it just long enough for Ella to grab it out of Firinne's mouth. She didn't have far to go since the boys had built a chain over half of the distance. She tried twice unsuccessfully to plant the pole in between the rocks under the water. The beams from the flashlights were pointed above the rapids so she could not see clearly into the darkness of the river. On her third try she wedged it securely. She flexed her legs and started toward Charlie; her eyes locked on his for moral support. Pushing off the pole, she reached for Charlie's outstretched hand. He grabbed her and locked arms, but Ella's grasp on the pole slipped. In a blink of an eye, the cheetah snatched the hickory stick and lunged onto the rocky ledge, next to Poppy. Poppy's eyes widened. She was impressed with Firinne's enormous muscular strength and accurate vision in the limited light. Poppy was able to reach out and grab Ella's hand. She completed the link across the river.

"It's your turn Mary," Firinne said gently.

Mary blinked twice and flashed a bright smile at the magnificent cheetah. She wasn't afraid. She was so excited to be an important part of the rescue team. Her adrenaline was racing and her heart swelled. The water was very high on her; just below her waist. She knew what she needed to do. She looked into each of their eyes as she curled her hands around their linked arms. She chose her steps wisely as she gripped this human chain, threading her way across the crashing water. Firinne stood on the edge, intently waiting to plunge into the rapids if Mary slipped. But she didn't. She crossed successfully and climbed up to the opposite side of the gorge, her heart racing with her success. The six friends remained planted

274

in the water, their arms linked. Firinne kept her focus on them, poised for a rescue if need be. Mary approached Eagla. Beside her sat a completely drenched shivering James. No one had noticed that he had thrown himself into the gorge and managed to swim to the other side. James stepped away from Mary and Eagla, and shook himself violently, trying to remove the water from his fur.

"No time to lose!" Eagla told Mary in a scratchy hoarse voice.

Eagla led Mary and James to the back of the cave. They were far away from the glow of the flashlights and in total darkness now. Mary's heightened hearing allowed her to follow the voices of the two cats, but the cheaters also lit the room with a bluish tinge, that somehow allowed her to see; but she could see more than the physical appearance of the cats. She could *see* or rather sense their emotions. Eagla exuded feelings of despair and dread, while James emitted feelings of hope and excitement. Mary shook her head, trying to focus on the task at hand. They approached what looked like the rear wall of the cave. The two cats crouched down and peered into a small crawl space under the rock wall.

"She's in there," croaked Eagla, peering at Mary with forlorn eyes.

Mary laid on her stomach and pulled her body into the opening, slithering on her belly, pulling at the rock floor with her fingers and the tips of her Mary Jane shoes. She was soaked from the rapids but none of that even registered in her brain right now. She could see the beautiful white owl, lying on her side breathing heavily, eyes closed. Searc had an aura of sadness around her.

"Searc" Mary whispered gently as she crawled toward the bird.

"Searc I'm here with Gra, to help bring you home." She spoke in a reassuring tone.

At the mention of Gra's name, Searc stirred and opened her eyes; her gaze upon Mary. Mary smiled at Searc.

"He loves you so much and he's been searching all of Chatterbox World for you. May I slide my wrist under you feathers?" Mary asked Searc politely.

"Yes please," whispered Searc, taking in the vision of this beautiful young child wearing Firinne's glasses. Searc wasn't quite sure if she was dreaming or if this was really happening.

Mary slid her wrist under Searc and gently held the bird in one hand, and then in both, as she wiggled her body out of the crawl space. She gently placed Searc on the floor of the cave, rolled over on her side and got to her feet. Searc focused on the slight young girl. Her legs and arms were scratched, her dress was wet and smeared with stone dust. Her face was dirty. The toothy grin and the look of absolute happiness that shone from her eyes behind the cheaters made her smile and chuckle. Searc's aura changed from sad to hopeful.

"Hurry Mary! Our legs are getting numb!" came a cry from the gorge.

"Do you have the strength to perch on my shoulder while I cross the water? Mary asked Searc.

"You don't have any other choice," James told Searc. "Give it all you've got."

Mary laid on the floor face down while Searc crawled onto her back. Searc entangled her talons into Mary's thick cascading curls. She tried not to touch the girl's skin. Searc leaned her face against Mary's cheek, using it to support herself. Her life was in this little girl's hands. Mary slowly stood up and approached the gorge. She crept down the embankment and made her way across the raging water for the second time. It was more awkward carrying Searc, but her confidence was now twofold. She plunged her feet into the water and swung from arm to arm. Firinne encouraged her and met her on the other side. Mary was shivering and exhausted when she reached Firinne but she was determined to finish alone. She crawled up the rocks and with a helpful boost in the butt from Firinne, collapsed safely onto the floor of the cavern.

"Bend your heads forward!" shouted James to the six friends still linked together in the water.

"I can't make it. Go on without me," Eagla said shaking her head sadly.

"Yes, you can! Go! Go! Make one more jump!" James shouted in Eagla's face.

"I'm too weak! I'll scratch them with my claws!"

"Jump you dumb cat!" bellowed Mike at the top of his lungs.

Eagla put every ounce of energy she had left in her body and lunged into the air. She completely missed Jibbs' back and landed on Mike, drawing blood from his neck.

"Hold on! Hold on with all you've got Eagla!" Mike screamed.

Jibbs motioned for James to jump onto his shoulder. After a successful landing, James wrapped his paws around Jibbs' neck, careful to keep his claws in. They left the roaring waters behind, as if they were a train chugging up a long steep mountain. Poppy pulled on Ella, who pulled on Charlie, who pulled on Finn, while Mike and Jibbs pushed from behind. They made their way to the edge of the water where they all collapsed in a disorderly pile. Mike held Eagla in his arms and sobbed tears of relief and exhaustion while he petted her bony damp head. Blood dripped down his back, matting his shirt to his skin but he didn't care. They were all safe on the right side of the river.

It was well past midnight when they reunited with Gra, left the cave and made the climb back to the field. They were greeted by Koko and the tinker. Finn helped Mary onto the back of Tinker's horse, Cobb. Gra and Searc rode in the tinker's wagon; along with Eagla, who was still wrapped in Mike's arms. The others walked. They made their way silently back to the log house. Everyone was too busy with their own thoughts and too exhausted to speak. They each fell asleep that night with the wild events of the day and their successful rescue of Gra's true love, swirling about in their dreams.

CHAPTER 28

THE TRUE NATURE OF EAGLA

The next day was warm and sunny with a light breeze. It was a day of recovery, and the mood changed to one of laughter and relief. They gathered outside, some on the porch and the others in the grassy field. Searc was doing well, thanks to the regenerating food and water from Tinker. In fact, everyone was looking much better. Eagla had taken a bath in one of the pools by the waterfall. She sat on Mike's lap while he dried her fur with a towel obtained from the tinker. She was enamored with Mike, staring up at his face, purring. It was very strange for his friends to watch as he sat in the sunshine stroking the cat's fur, talking and laughing.

"Something weird happened to that boy in those caves," said Charlie shaking his head.

"Something happened to *all* of us in those caves." agreed Poppy, her eyes lingering on Mary. Mary stood in the field surrounded by scattered wildflowers, shading her eyes from the sun while watching Searc gain her strength back with a short flight. Poppy's attention refocused on Koko. She laughed quietly at his antics. He was performing multiple backflips; showing off in front of Firinne. Jibbs was sitting on the ground, propped against the cheetah, rubbing his face against Firinne's spots while he gently massaged her neck. He loved the cheetah. She made him feel calm and strong.

"I think it's time we hear Searc's story of how she came to be in the cavern crawl space in the depths of the Geata Waterfall," said James, as he emerged from a patch of tall grasses.

"Are you ready to tell your tale?" asked Gra, when Searc returned from her flight. "Or do you need more time?"

"I am happy to tell my tale to my wonderful friends and rescuers," she said, perching on the front porch railing of the little house. They all crowded around to listen.

"I went for my usual twilight flight," she began, nodding toward Gra. *"It was a beautiful evening with just a slight breeze and a moonlit sky. The storm erupted so quickly it took me off guard. A bolt of lightning hit the tree I was flying over and some of the residual electricity must have surged through my body. Between that and the driving rain, I plummeted down into Geata Waterfall. I crashed among the rocky ledges below, injuring my wing, but luckily missing the surge of water. I lost consciousness and when I awoke, I was being dragged by one of my talons into the cave. I panicked. I didn't realize that Eagla was actually pulling me to safety. I was crazy with fear and confusion and I managed to fly further and further down into the caves, using only my one wing. I was delirious by the time I reached the area where you found me."*

"How did you ever make it by the low arch in the cave?" Gra interrupted.

"I really don't know. My adrenaline was raging and I had lost control of my reasoning. I am sure that I hit the water at some point, because my feathers were drenched and I could barely move, when I dragged myself into the crawl space and passed out. I don't know how long I was unconscious, but when I awoke, Eagla was curled up beside me, keeping me warm, and had brought me a few mice to munch on. Once she saw that I was still able to take nourishment, she actually voluntarily soaked herself in the gorge so that I could slurp water from her dripping coat of fur. I owe my life to Eagla. She stayed by my side for days.... well, until you rescued me."

Gra looked at the scraggly, striped cat, feeling embarrassed that he had allowed himself to look upon her with disdain in the past; his opinion of her, swayed by the idle gossip and rumors he heard among the woodland animals. He had never spent time with Eagla. He had not tried to help her or guide her in any way. He had made a terrible mistake. Firinne stared intently at Eagla and hung her head in shame. James approached the black and grey striped heroine and sat beside her. She had the same build as James, but she was thin and worn looking from years of living in the rough. Eagla had beautiful emerald eyes that looked enormous in her skinny frame. She confidently wore a small bite out of her tail, several patches of missing fur on her back and a few impressive battle scars on her belly. Eagla took great pride in the fact that she had survived on her own and been able to defend herself from some very fierce opponents in Pernicious Woods. She was one tough cat.

Gra fluttered off the railing and met with Eagla face to face.

"Eagla, I apologize to you on behalf of myself, and all those who have judged you so wrongly in the past. I am forever in your debt. I will be honored to help you in any way I can in the future. You will never go hungry or be without shelter again."

"Aww, what's the fun in that! Sounds pretty boring to me!" she said with a crooked smirk.

Everyone laughed.

James affectionately bumped foreheads with Eagla.

"I'll take some more of that water if you don't mind Mr. Tinker," Eagla said. "That stuff makes me feel like I've just downed three mice and inhaled a whole rain puddle!"

Mary jumped up and filled a saucer from the kitchen full of the tinker's magical water. She rubbed her forehead with her hands and squinted in pain as she watched Eagla lick the bowl dry.

"It's the glasses," said Firinne.

"I know, they make my head ache if I wear them too long," answered Mary.

Mary removed the glasses from her face and her headache immediately disappeared. Poppy tapped the back of Mary's hand and took the cheaters, placing them back into her overall bib pocket. She took Mary's hand and led her to the porch steps. They sat down together and Mary rested her head on Poppy's shoulder. Eagla abandoned her empty bowl and curled into Mary's lap for a snooze. It was comforting to Mary to stroke Eagla's fur. It kept her mind off losing her sight so suddenly. She had worn the glasses all morning and was getting used to seeing as others do....as others take for granted.

"Where do we go from here?" asked Finn, looking at the tinker.

"Where do you want to go from here?" he answered, staring intently into Finn's eyes.

"Well, we have to find our way home at some point; although I feel it will be so sad to leave Chatterbox World and our friends," he said with a slight blur of water in his eyes.

Tinker smiled at Finn.

"Once you have been in Chatterbox World, it becomes part of your world back home. You will take your memories, the love of your friends, and the things you have learned, home with you. You can choose to stay or go home, whatever you like."

"Will we ever be able to come back again if we leave?" Ella asked Tinker, with a lump in her throat.

"That depends," answered the tinker cocking his head to one side.

"It depends on what?" Poppy chimed in with some pep in her tone.

"A lot of things…." said Tinker. "Usually the only way to *enter* Chatterbox World is if you are needed and invited. Something tells me that you will all be welcome in this world for the rest of your lives. You have made it a better place than it was before you entered. Very few beings, especially humans, have the ability to do that. Most have the tendency to strip the world and take for themselves. If you remain kind of heart and treat others like you would like to be treated, the door to Chatterbox World will always be open for you."

"Koko and I stay," said Jibbs with a happy smile.

"I am very pleased to hear that. You and Koko are very welcome and respected in Chatterbox World. Few others have been able to successfully navigate the Pernicious Woods, gain the mutual respect of some of its most feared creatures, and navigate their very strict code of ethics. Koko grinned his happy face smile. Jibbs simply glanced at the tinker. Tinker cleared his throat. The corners of his mouth twitched slightly and a smile appeared in his eyes.

"You truly are a wonderful guy," he said grinning at Jibbs.

Happy tears started to trickle down Jibbs' face.

"Time to go swimming!" he shouted as he and Koko headed toward Gaeta Waterfall.

Poppy and a few others wiped tears from their eyes.

"I would like to go home, to see my friend Tim before he leaves. I need to be with my father and help him run the grist mill as best as I can." said Mary.

"*Grist mill,*" mused Eagla perking up. "Your world seems interesting; I might like to try a new change of scenery. May I go with you Mary?"

"Yes Eagla! I'd love that!" Mary answered excitedly. "Is that okay Tinker?"

"Eagla may do as she pleases; and of course, she may return anytime she likes." Tinker said with a wink at the striped cat.

"I do miss Mamo so much," Poppy said longingly.

Finn, Ella, Charlie and Mike all agreed that it was time to go home. Poppy tapped the back of Mary's hand. She slid the cheaters into Mary's open palm.

"In case you need them from time to time," Poppy whispered into Mary's ear as she hugged her tightly.

This time Mary tapped Poppy on the back of *her* hand. Poppy flipped her hand over. Mary placed her little wooden chicken into Poppy's palm and closed her fingers around it. "This is for you Poppy; to remember me."

"But you need your chicken!" Poppy protested.

"I don't think I really do anymore," answered Mary with a smile.

With that comment, she was gone.

She and Eagla just disappeared before everyone's eyes.

Poppy's eyes filled with tears. She turned to look at Gra and all her wonderful friends, to somehow say goodbye to them, but she was spared this heart-wrenching task. She was no longer sitting on the front porch of the log house. Ella, Finn, Mike Charlie and Poppy were now all sitting on the floor of the octagonal cabin, in the world from which they had come.

CHAPTER 29

DIFFERENT WORLD DIFFERENT TIME ALL COMBINE TO MAKE LIFE DEVINE

T he sound of Poppy's voice became distant and the feel of Poppy's hand in hers began to fade away. The noises of Chatterbox World were gone. The grass in front of her had turned into a wooden floor; one that she knew and felt at home with. Mary was sitting on the floor of her little octagonal playhouse; the one that her father and Timothy had made for her. Eagla was still curled up in her lap and she clutched the cheaters in her hand. The chatterbox was on the floor next to her. Mary stood and placed the cheaters in her desk drawer; the one with the cat tail handle. They were useless in this world; besides, she had seen everything she really needed to see. She took a tiny bag of Tinker's magic seeds from her dress pocket and placed them in one of the little secret drawers at the back of the desk. Mary then placed the chatterbox into the little domed top trunk. She kept everything she owned always in the same place, so she could find it again. She already missed her wonderful new friends, but somehow, she knew that she would see them again someday. There was a light knock on the door. Timothy entered the room.

"Mary it's time for dinner. Maggie has made your favorite!"

Her heart pounded at the sound of Timothy's voice.

She ran to him and hugged him around the waist, fighting back tears of joy.

"I found this cat. She really needs a home. Can we keep her?"

Mary's father had allowed her to keep Eagla. The cat became strong again and very healthy; her fur soft and luxurious. Most of her scars were covered with new thick black and grey stripes. But the few that remained kept the neighborhood feline bullies away. Over the years, Eagla became very attached and completely devoted to Mary and Timothy. She was still very feisty, but she had people who loved her and took care of her; and feisty is ok as long as it is mixed with love.

Mary would enjoy the time she had left with Timothy. Although life would bring her both great happiness and sadness, she now had the courage and strength and self-confidence to move forward.

****

"We're back!" Ella said.

Toby jumped from one to another, licking their faces and wagging his tail.

"I feel soooo weird," said Charlie rubbing his eyes.

Finn watched Poppy place the chatterbox back into the little domed trunk. She placed the key in the middle drawer of the desk; the one with the cat tail handle. She caught her breath. The cheaters were in the drawer.

"They're all gone," said Mike sadly. "We'll never see Mary or Eagla……"

"Huh! That's what *you* think!" said James with a smirk.

No one had noticed him perched on the top of the antique sewing machine.

"James!" shouted Poppy.

They all crowded around the giant orange striped feline.

"Well you better get back before you're missed!" said James with a look of impatience. "Go!"

They laughed at the pushiness of the cat and headed to the door. Poppy turned back to smile and wave goodbye to James, but he was gone.

"Come on Pops let's go" Finn said.

"Wait!" she told the group. "Finn, we have to tell Mamo the truth; tell her about the cabin and

Chatterbox World. We can't just go on and never say anything. It will be too hard and I don't want to lie to Mamo."

"You're right Pops, but how is she ever going to believe us?"

"I'm bringing the chatterbox with us. I'll show it to her," she said unlocking the little trunk. Poppy gingerly placed the chatterbox in her backpack and they left the cabin behind.

"What are we going to say to Mamo and Seamus?" Ella asked Finn and Poppy. We don't even know how long we've been gone."

"I'm probably going to be grounded for the summer!" Mike said sighing.

"I'm sure my mom has called the police by now," Charlie nodded, his eyes wide with the thought.

"We have no other choice. We just have to go home and see," Finn said, linking his arm with Poppy's.

Ella grabbed Poppy's other arm and they made their way back through the dark woods. They were surprised to see their tents were still set up by the riverside. Suddenly Poppy missed Mamo and Seamus so much, that she broke free of Ella and Finn and bolted across the field toward her home. They all arrived at the back-porch screen door and peered inside. They crowded in closely to see if she was alone. Mamo was seated at the kitchen table.

Across from her was Mr. Timpiste. They were enjoying a small plate of Mr. Timpiste's cookies.

"That was a wonderful dinner Timothy," Mamo said.

"I had a great time too Mary," Mr. Timpiste answered, reaching for her hand. He held her delicate fingers in his and gazed lovingly at his lifelong friend. In all these years, he thought, she had never lost her beauty. Her eyes, though they were blind, were still a brilliant blue and full of happiness and the love of her family and friends.

Poppy, Finn, Ella, Mike and Charlie stood stone still, peering into the screen door. They stood in the darkness in complete shock. Their minds were racing. They had never heard Mr. Timpiste and Mamo address each other by their first names before. Maybe they had, but they didn't notice. Poppy looked at Finn, her mouth and eyes open wide. Finn returned the look nodding his head yes. It all made sense. Ella looked at Mike and Charlie.

"Did you just hear that?" she whispered to Mike.

"This can't be real," Mike shook his head no.

"What can't be real?" Charlie shouted.

Mary and Timothy looked toward the screen door. Timothy, that is, Mr. Timpiste peered out into the darkness.

"Hey! It's the kids! Come on in and have some cookies with us!"

They all filed into the kitchen. They didn't say a word, just looked at Mr. Timpiste and then at Mamo.

"How you all doing? You decide not to camp out by the river tonight?" Mamo asked with a laugh.

Silence

"Are any of you hungry?" she asked a little curiously. She was not sure why they were being so quiet.

"What's up with you kids? The cat got your tongue?"

"Mamo, is your name Mary?" Poppy asked her grandmother very seriously.

"Why yes, Poppy. You know that," she said reaching out for Poppy's hand. Poppy crossed the room and took Mamo's hand in hers.

Poppy began to sob. They were tears of relief, happiness, shock, all mixed together. Through her tears she turned to Mr. Timpiste and said: "Mr. Timpiste, are you Timothy?"

Mamo and Mr. Timpiste were quite surprised that the kids had come back from camping to ask them what their given names were. Mr. Timpiste looked at Mamo, a little confused, trying to see if this meant anything to her.

"Why yes Poppy, my given name is Timothy."

Poppy wriggled out of her backpack and gently removed the chatterbox. She tapped Mamo on the back of her hand and then placed the chatterbox into Mamo's open palm. Mamo felt the smooth surface of the chatterbox. She slipped her fingers in between the triangles and felt it slip open. Her face turned white and her beautiful blue unseeing eyes opened wide.

"Oh my! Oh, my Poppy! Finn! Ella! Mike and Charlie, are you here?"

"Yes, Mamo we're all here," said Finn gazing at his grandmother in a whole new light.

"You've found my chatterbox!" she said shaking her head with disbelief and laughter.

Timothy Timpiste sat very still, his hands on his forehead, staring at the chatterbox.

"Now *that* brings back some memories!" he said.

After the initial shock that Mamo and Mary were one in the same and Mr. Timpiste was her lifelong friend, Timothy, there was a feeling of relief and happiness in the room. They chattered on and on about their adventures.

It all felt very surreal. Many of the details that had faded for Mamo, came to light. She laughed and cried and bathed herself in the happiness that it brought to her, to remember her adventures in Chatterbox World.

Finn had a question for Mamo.

"Wasn't it strange that mom named us Poppy and Finn; the same names as your friends from Chatterbox World?"

"Well no Finn, not really. I, of course, had grown to love those names, and played a big part in naming you and your sister. Since your mother liked my suggestions and loved the names as well…. but I *did* wonder from time to time when you made friends with Ella, Mike and Charlie. I questioned myself. I wondered sometimes, if I had dreamt up Chatterbox World. I mean how could it all be true? It was all so long ago…. a lifetime ago, when I was a child; before Timothy joined the Air Force."

"Yeah, it really is an awful lot to explain to someone," Finn said with a laugh. "I'm *very* glad we didn't have to try to explain it to you!"

"I still don't know what's actually going on," said Charlie shaking his head, looking confused.

"I'll explain it later Stubbs," said Mike.

Ella put her hand to her mouth and giggled, "Oh Charlie!"

Poppy started giggling too.

"Wait!" said Poppy, running to Mamo. "I have something of yours!"

She slipped her hand into her overall bib pocket and pulled out Chicken. She tapped Mamo on the back of her hand.

"It's Chicken!" said Poppy with a toothy smile.

Mamo felt the soft worn wood of Chicken between her fingers. She held it to her face. Tears filled her eyes and she pulled Poppy close to her.

"I love you Poppy. I love all of you kids with all my heart. You are my past, my life and my future. You make living worthwhile!"

"Well!" said Mr. Timpiste. "It looks like I finally made a chicken who **wanted** to be a chicken!

They all laughed and agreed with Mr. Timpiste.

Mike, Charlie and Ella slept over that night. They had so many questions for Mamo and Mr. Timpiste. Mamo promised, that Timothy would rejoin them for breakfast the next morning to further discuss their adventures, if they went to bed. The next morning, after lots of reminiscing about their friends from Chatterbox World, they sat together happily enjoying breakfast.

"What ever happened to Eagla?" Mike asked Mamo in between bites of toast.

"Well, she's currently sleeping in the bay window of my workshop," Mr. Timpiste answered Mike.

"What!!" Mike shouted.

"How is that possible!?" Finn asked, thinking about the sleepy cat he had petted so many times. "She must be ancient!"

"Well, she's from Chatterbox World and appears to have her own timeline. She never seems to get any older.... or less feisty!"

They all laughed.

Poppy, Ella, Finn, Charlie and Mike spent the rest of the summer cleaning and fixing up the old grist mill. Seamus joined in and worked with the boys to clear the river and start the great water wheel. Mr. Timpiste and Finn cleaned and repaired the magnificent wall clock in the mill office.

On a beautiful day in August, Finn and Poppy walked on either side of Mamo, leading her through the field, over the bridge and into the woods to visit the playhouse she had loved more than fifty years ago. She felt the cat faces on the front of the desk and lovingly touched Mr. Timpiste's pinned stories. Her fingers wrapped around the miniature bag of tiny seeds that Tinker had given to her so long ago. Poppy placed her hand on the loosened brick in the tunnel that housed her wooden animals. Mamo loved feeling the shapes of the cow, pig and giraffe that Timothy had carved for her. She laughed and cried a little, remembering the wonderful times she had as a child at the mill. They met up with Ernie and Mr. Timpiste, Seamus, Mike and Charlie, in the grist mill office. Everyone's favorite moment was when Poppy wound the crank on Mamo's little Victrola. Mamo, Ella and Poppy danced around the office holding hands, singing and laughing. Too embarrassed to dance, Mike, Charlie and Finn, jammed their hands into their pockets and jumped around the room singing "You Are My Sunshine!" at the top of their lungs.

They sat on the river bank eating sandwiches Mamo had made that morning.

"You have all made me so very happy. Although I cannot see your faces today......I still remember what you looked like all those years ago.... how you made me feel useful, important, necessary.... you gave me hope. Although we parted on that sunny day in Chatterbox World, you all came back to me.... even my sweet Timothy."

"And Chicken!" added Charlie enthusiastically. "Don't forget your chicken…he came back to you too!"

Everyone laughed.

Finn, much to Ella's delight, was holding her hand again. He whispered into her ear:

"Do you think Charlie gets it now?"

"I doubt it," Ella laughed.

CHAPTER 30

A COLORFUL WORLD OF
TALKING CATS

This was it. The first day of sixth grade, and Poppy was excited. Her bus dropped her off in front of the school, where Ella was waiting for her.

"Queasy stomach?" Ella asked.

"No way!" Poppy grinned. "Bring it on!"

Poppy was in the homeroom next to Ella. She and everyone else in the room could hear laughter coming from next door. Poppy and a couple of the other kids snuck out of the room and peeked into Ella's, to see what was so funny. Gwenn Grotty,

Bonnie Craven and Karlyn Keister were squirming in their seats, red faced and embarrassed. Karlyn's hair was bright purple, Bonnie's was blue and Gwenn's was neon green. Poppy and Ella locked eyes and joined in on the laughter. They just couldn't help it.

"How did this wonderful thing happen?" thought Poppy as she returned to her homeroom.

After school, Finn and Poppy sat in the living room watching T.V. Poppy told Finn about Gwenn, Bonnie and Karlyn's hair. Finn had seen the girls in school.

"I mean, they were pretty hard to miss!" he said with a laugh.

Mamo walked into the room.

"I guess they really liked the cookies Mr. Timpiste and I made for them."

"What!!!" Poppy and Finn said together.

"Well, Mr. Timpiste and I went over to chat with Gwenn's mother about how things were going in school. Mrs. Grotty was in complete denial that her daughter would ever pick on anyone. She was quite rude and slammed the door in our face; but not before she had taken the box of cookies we made for her family. I brought the cookies, to let them know there would be no hard feelings as long as the girls learned to behave themselves," Mamo said with a smile.

Poppy and Finn were both shocked and *so* proud of Mamo all at once.

"Hmmm, even stranger than that…." Finn said, "Mike was telling me that everyone at school, was talking about how Gwen and her side-kicks, were claiming Mr. Timpiste's cat had threatened them, and told them never to walk by Mr. Timpiste's house or Contraption Rehab again."

Poppy shook her head, laughed, and said;

"Wow that's embarrassing. *Everyone* knows cats can't talk!"

THE END

Made in the USA
Middletown, DE
09 November 2018